THE BOY JACKO

Peter Dawlish

James Lennox Kerr

THE BOY JACKO

Illustrated by

WILLIAM STOBBS

FRANKLIN WATTS, INC.
575 Lexington Avenue, New York 22

Contents

SUMMONS TO VIRGINIA

As always, Lawyer Burdell gazed on his nephew without pleasure. The fourteen-year-old boy, Matthew Tuke, standing across a table from his uncle, flushed guiltily, and put a hand down to hide the tear in his grey cloth breeches. The tear, with a bruise under his left eye and a smear of mud on a cheek, was a trophy of the game of football Matt had just come from, and the boy told himself he should have got rid of this evidence before coming before his uncle. Usually, Matt managed to steal into the house after a game to find his Aunt Janet, who would tut-tut over his condition, but mend torn clothing and attend to cuts and bruises before the boy met his uncle at a meal, the only time the lawyer sat with his family. Today, however, the message brought to Matt by his cousin Peter had been too important and exciting for the boy to think of his appearance, or his uncle's disapproval of rough games and the company of the city's more unruly lads. He had raced for home as quickly as he could, bursting into the room his uncle described as his 'chambers' and where the lawyer conducted a meagre law practice, only to bring up against the table and be greeted with the familiar cold disapproval. Now, Matt thought ruefully, he would be lectured, reminded that he came from a respectable household and had at least been born a gentleman; and that he disgraced both home and name by joining in the wild football games that ranged through the streets of Exeter and sent respectable citizens scurrying from the horde of yelling, kicking, and struggling men and boys. Matt had heard the lecture dozens of times before, ever since he had been brought to his uncle's home after his parents died when he was eight years of age. Now he lowered his head submissively, glancing once at the stranger who sat near the table and then at the papers under his uncle's thin hand.

This time, to Matt's surprise the lecture was not delivered. Instead, after the little cough he always gave before speaking, the lawyer turned round the papers he held and pushed them towards the boy.

'A letter has come from your Uncle Franklyn,' the man said coldly, 'summoning you to Virginia.' He held up a hand as Matt exclaimed, then went on, 'This . . .' The lawyer hesitated, frowning slightly as he glanced at the stranger, then said, 'This officer has come to escort you to Bristol, where you are to go aboard a ship sailing for Virginia.'

'Your uncle flatters me, sir,' the stranger said apologetically, 'I am captain's clerk aboard the ship *Speedwell*. Captain Howell has sent me to deliver these letters and to carry you to him. He is busy gathering a cargo for the voyage.'

Matt grinned at the man, not caring what position he held and only delighted that the stranger was the means of taking him to his Uncle Franklyn. He noticed the man was neatly dressed in dark-coloured coat and breeches, and that he wore a short-haired well-curled brown wig tied at his neck with a thin black ribbon. The face under the wig was thin and strangely pale for a seafarer, the eyes small and shrewd as they examined the boy.

'My name is Parker, sir,' the man added,—'Daniel Parker.'

'A pleasure, sir,' Matt said, his smile wide and friendly. 'When do we sail for Virginia?'

The man shrugged his shoulders.

'Captain Howell hopes to be away from Bristol in a fortnight from now,' he answered. 'I am instructed to have you aboard in the next ten days.'

'The boy has to have clothes,' Lawyer Burdell interrupted. 'Colonel Tuke wishes him to be suitably equipped for his new life. My wife is now preparing a list of what will be required.'

There was jealousy and bitterness in the lawyer's voice and Parker glanced at him quickly. He sounded as though he grudged this lad his good fortune in becoming the protégé and heir of a wealthy planter. Captain Howell of the ship *Speedwell* was an intimate friend of Colonel Franklyn Tuke, and the clerk had heard the two men discussing this boy and Colonel Tuke's plans for him. The retired soldier had remained loyal to King James, had fought for him, and had had to flee the country when William, Prince of Orange, became king in 1688. After the defeat of King James's army in Ireland, Colonel Tuke had gone to Virginia, where he had bought and developed a large tobacco plantation. He was now one of the richest and most influential men in the colony, and to be his heir was a glittering prospect for any lad. This young fellow, who looked like some farm lad and stood grinning like an idiot, would find himself far out of his depth in the planter's magnificent mansion outside Williamsburg, and among the colonial gentlemen who lived like kings. The clerk's shrewd eyes had missed nothing of the poverty in this lawyer's home, and he knew the other man's history. Lawyer Burdell—whose wife was Colonel Tuke's sister—had also backed the wrong horse in King James, though less gallantly than the soldier. It was enough, however, to lose him the new Court's favour, and also the handling of the affairs of those courtiers who had fled with their king. He had had to leave his prosperous practice in London and had come to Exeter, where, obviously, he had not prospered. West Country people had no liking for strangers and Lawyer Burdell was not the sort to become popular anywhere. Parker, envious of this boy's good fortune himself, could understand the lawyer's jealousy. But the man was a fool to show his dislike for his nephew. He should conceal his envy and make much of the boy, and profit in the future. Daniel Parker, the clerk told himself, would have played his cards more cleverly, and this simple-faced lad was the sort who would be grateful for any friendliness, generous in his gratitude. A man would do well to play up to him.

A sound behind Matt brought him round, to greet his cousin, who had returned after delivering the summons that had brought Matt home.

'Peter,' Matt cried, delightedly, 'I am for Virginia at last. Uncle Franklyn has sent for me.'

He waited for his cousin's handsome features to show he shared Matt's pleasure, but Peter only shrugged his shoulders inside the neat coat he wore, evading the other boy's eyes.

'I congratulate you on your good fortune, cousin,' he said primly, but with a sourness in his voice that brought a flush to Matt's cheeks and a quick glance from the ship's clerk.

Matt was embarrassed, remembering that Peter was not to share this great adventure, but had to stay here in Exeter and, when his schooling was over, find some position in a merchant's office, or another humble place. Matt was suddenly sorry for the other boy.

'I will tell Uncle Franklyn to send for you also, Peter,' he exclaimed eagerly. 'He will find you a position and you will make your fortune.'

Peter did not respond, except to turn away and move nearer a wall of the room. Parker almost smiled, then did not. Instead he turned to Lawyer Burdell.

'You will pardon me, sir,' he said in a soft, insinuating voice, 'but would it not be best that the young gentleman be fitted out in Bristol? His uncle, Colonel Tuke, moves in the highest society in Williamsburg, and it may be that Exeter tailors are not acquainted with the newest fashions.'

The clerk's suggestion was greeted without pleasure, by a haughty lifting of the lawyer's head.

'There are excellent tailors here in Exeter,' he said coldly, 'and also, he has to have shirts and such things that his aunt will see to. He need not leave for another week and I will arrange with a tailor at once.'

Parker's expression did not change. He inclined his head, accepting the rebuff. But his eyes gleamed with annoyance. Colonel Tuke had sent over a generous sum to outfit his nephew and Parker had thought to have a few pickings. Now, the clerk thought spitefully, this sour-faced lawyer would make something out of equipping the boy. The uncle and his family were about to lose a profitable lodger, for the planter paid generously for his nephew's keep. Judging by the poor furnishings of this room, the money would be missed. The clerk felt like shrugging his thin shoulders, and there was only half-concealed scorn in his eyes when he looked up again. Let the lawyer make his few pence, but Daniel Parker would have made better use of the lad. The clerk's shrewd brain was already considering how he might insinuate himself into Matt's good fortune, maybe get the boy to like him, and invite him ashore, to some good position with the planter. The boy looked like a fool and there was wealth in this business. Parker would keep his eyes watchful for an opportunity to share Matt's new-found prosperity.

The man rose as a woman came into the room, a slightly built, worried-looking woman who was gazing at Matt fondly and with sadness in her eyes. The boy was grinning at her.

'You know, Aunt Janet?' he cried.

'Yes, pet,' the woman answered. 'I did not think to lose you so soon.'

The boy laughed and went to her side, putting an arm round her affectionately.

'It is time I went,' he said happily. 'I waste my time at school, for I am a blockhead and cannot learn anything. I'll be better at fighting redskins and growing tobacco.'

His aunt turned to her husband.

'I have read the list brother Franklyn sent,' she said. 'It is a prodigious lot, and I will require two girls to assist me. A week is too short a time for all that must be made. And you must buy the stockings. They have to be of best silk.'

Matt laughed again, delight in his eyes.

'I to wear silk stockings, Aunt Janet?' he cried in pretended horror. 'I'd sooner have what you knit for me. Let us buy the others for Peter. He loves such finery.'

'Aye, silk, my love,' his aunt said tenderly, 'and silk and velvet for your coats and breeches.' She turned to Parker, 'Is this not so, sir?'

The clerk bowed slightly, glancing down at his own silk-encased calves and the fine cloth of his breeches.

'It is so, Madam,' he agreed. 'The young gentleman is to move in circles where fashion is important. Your brother, Colonel Tuke, lives in great state.'

Matt groaned, but he was smiling broadly.

'I begin to wish it were Peter and not me who is to go to Virginia,' he said, humorously rueful. 'I had thought to be at work all day, or fighting savages.' He looked at Parker anxiously, 'Is Virginia so settled now, Master Parker? Are there no redskins to fight with?'

The man smiled, flattering the boy with his eyes. 'That, I am sure, you would do bravely, sir,' he said. 'But they are all driven into the interior now. Where your uncle is, some twenty miles outside Williamburg, the country is settled, with all you will find here in England. Williamsburg is already a handsome town, with the governor's palace, and even a college which you can attend.'

'I've had enough schooling,' Matt retorted. He sighed his disappointment with the peacefulness of the colony. 'Ah, well,' he comforted himself, 'perhaps we will encounter a few pirates on the voyage.'

His uncle interrupted then, speaking impatiently.

'You will go with your aunt now,' he said, 'and she will measure you for your new shirts. I will call on a tailor and arrange for him to come here.'

The boy grinned at his aunt.

'Come then, Aunt Janet,' he said. 'Let's get it over with.'

They left the room and the lawyer turned to the ship's clerk.

'My son will escort you to an inn where you can lodge, Master Parker,' he said coldly. 'I am afraid my house lacks space for your comfort.' He turned to the boy standing across the room. 'Peter,' he said, 'you will take Master Parker to the Blue Anchor. That is a mariners' tavern.'

The clerk's eyes gleamed with dislike as he bowed, hating the lawyer for the insult of placing him with common sailors. But he said nothing, waiting until the lawyer had placed his tricorn hat on his wig and had stalked from the room. Then Parker turned to look more searchingly at Peter, examining him shrewdly. He saw a boy almost Matt's height, but slimmer and a great deal neater in appearance. Something of a fop, the man decided, noting the care Peter had taken with his brown locks, the attempts to smarten his cheap clothing. There was a discontented scowl on the handsome face, for Peter disliked his task of escorting the visitor.

'I do not know the Blue Anchor,' the boy said stiffly and haughtily. 'It is somewhere by the canal, I suppose, where the ships come.'

Parker smiled, not even pretending humility in front of this young sprig.

'Do not let that trouble you,' he said. 'I am already lodged. My horse and gear are at the Mermaid Inn.'

Peter's eyes opened wider.

'I can guide you there, sir,' he said more respectfully. 'It is the best inn in Exeter.'

'That is why I lodge there,' Parker answered, glancing round the room scornfully. 'Your father mistakes my rank.'

'My father knows nothing of mariners,' Peter said meekly, impressed by the man's manner. 'And he cannot forget that we were once rich and of better condition.'

Nor can you, my boy, the clerk decided. A chip off the old block, if I know one, and envious of the other lad's good fortune. The clerk took his hat from the table and then smiled at the boy. He would have sport with this young prig; show him that Daniel Parker could act the gentleman with anyone.

'Come, then,' he said, mocking the boy, 'and you will sup with me tonight. I had thought to invite your father, but he is too stiff-necked for my liking. You will make better company.'

Peter's cheeks flushed and his eyes brightened with pleasure. To sup at the Mermaid! He could boast to his schoolmates tomorrow, crow over his cousin.

'Should you have your mother's permission?' the man asked, still mocking the boy. Peter raised his head disdainfully.

'I do as I please, sir,' he boasted, 'and I am delighted to sup with you.'

The man hid his amusement. This was a vain fool and would be an entertainment for the evening. He went to the door, followed by Peter, both of them being elaborately polite and aping what they were sure were the manners of gentlemen. Peter was delighted with himself, for this was his idea of an adventure, and he was quite sure he was impressing the man. At the inn Parker ordered their supper, calling for a bottle of wine in a loud voice, and Peter knew himself to be where he really ought to be. He recognized several of the city's notables at other tables and thought of how he would make his school-mates jealous tomorrow. He drank the wine Parker poured, and his glass was immediately refilled. He boasted, the man encouraging him to talk, and soon Peter was describing how he should have been mixing with the highest in London and what a fool his father had been to support King James. The boy's voice rose shrilly, drawing curious glances from the other guests, but Parker was enjoying himself. It satisfied his spite against the lawyer to make the son look foolish before others, and the man saw to it that Peter's glass was kept filled. The boy talked more, telling how he did not intend to remain in Exeter, but would go to London and make his fortune. His mother, he complained, could have helped him long since, but she would not appeal to those of her old friends who were still in high positions. But he would approach them, and use their patronage. The boy had a dozen schemes for making his fortune and placing himself where his birth entitled him to be. Parker let him boast, thoroughly enjoying himself.

'A lad like you, Peter,' he agreed slyly, 'you're too smart to stay in a place like Exeter. Now if it were you I carried to Virginia, you would make a proper figure there.'

Peter scowled, reminded of his cousin's good fortune.

'You are right, sir,' he said resentfully. 'Matt disgraces our family with his roughness and love for low company. He would rather be with boxers and wrestlers than in genteel company and has no interest in genteel pursuits.' The boy, his envy unconcealed as the wine affected him, looked across the table bitterly. 'It is wicked of Uncle Franklyn to send for Matt,' he went on, 'because Matt is an orphan. What fortune can I have with such parents as mine, but to be clerk to some merchant?'

'A shame indeed, Peter,' the man agreed sympathetically, 'and you lose much. Your uncle is one of the richest men in Virginia and lives like a nobleman. His mansion has some twenty rooms, with dozens of slaves to wait on him and some hundred others working on his plantation. I fear me your cousin will be like a bull among china in such magnificence.'

Peter could have wept as he listened.

'He has not the qualities for such a position,' he said contemptuously. 'He is not even interested in fashion. . . . Did ye hear him when mother said he had to have silk stockings? I hate worsted and the poor clothes I have to wear.'

'It is very sad,' Parker said, hiding his amusement, 'that such a fortune and high position goes to one who would rather toil as a labourer.'

'That is all Matt is fitted for,' the other said spitefully. 'Why, I have even to write his letters to Uncle Franklyn, for he is better with an oar or a cricket bat than a pen.'

The man's eyebrows lifted.

'You write his letters, Peter?' he asked softly. 'Can he not write?'

'Like a babe scrawling in the mud,' Peter answered scornfully. 'Our schoolmaster has caned him fifty times for inattention and stupidity. He is absent from his lessons often, going off with the rogues round the ships, or chasing a fox somewhere. He has his own horse, for Uncle Franklyn would have him a rider with the hounds.' The boy's voice trailed into self-pity as he went on: 'While I am scarcely permitted to use my father's old nag.'

Parker answered the boy absently, for he was thinking, turning over in his mind what Peter had said about writing Matt's letters to Colonel Tuke. The ship's clerk was an opportunist, always seeking how he could profit by people's weakness, or by some clever trick. Until now, his gains had been merely what he could make by petty cheating in his buying of stores for the ship, by taking bribes from ships' chandlers or by selling anything he thought Captain Howell would not miss. But he had always dreamed of a great *coup,* of an opportunity to make a fortune by some smart piece of trickery, and he had been searching for some way to use this mission he was on for his own advantage. He had thought to make a little profit by outfitting Matt, but the boy's uncle had spoiled that chance; though Parker did the lawyer an injustice in believing he would cheat his nephew or brother-in-law. Lawyer Burdell had only hoped that by taking business to a tailor or haberdasher he might find a client; he would not have considered petty thievery. Had Parker known this, he would have given the lawyer no praise, only scorn for not making something out of the buying of his nephew's outfit.

The clerk had considered working himself into Matt's good opinion, making the boy grateful by doing small services and flattering him, but the man was shrewd enough to see that this was not the sort of boy who could be flattered. He was far from being bright, but he would be the sort to prefer directness and recognize honesty in people. Parker was fairly certain that he would not impress the boy, and once aboard the *Speedwell* would see little of him. Matt would be Captain Howell's guest and would require nothing from a lowly clerk. No other scheme had occurred to Parker, until now, when Peter mentioned that he always had written Matt's letters to Colonel Tuke. Then an idea, startling in its daring, had come to the clerk, and his guest was no longer something to amuse him. He could be the means to fortune. The now half-drunken boy was startled and bewildered by Parker breaking into his tale of woe with a question.

'Tell me, Peter,' the man was asking eagerly, 'has Colonel Tuke ever seen you or your cousin?'

The boy frowned, shaking his head and trying to think through the wine haze in his brain.

'He sailed for Virginia long before we were born,' he said at last. 'After King James was defeated in Ireland. I have heard my mother talk of this. I was not born until some years after my uncle fled, and Matt is six months younger than I am.'

'Your uncle has never returned to England?' Parker went on quickly.

'He dare not,' Peter told him, 'or he would be sent to the Tower of London.'

The man breathed a soft 'Ah . . .', then looked at the boy keenly. He was near enough Matt's size, though slimmer. His

B.J.—B

hair was a lighter shade of brown than his cousin's, his face prettier, if with less character. There was a ruggedness in Matt that this boy lacked, but unless a pen was very skilful a written description of one would be near enough to the other.

'Has your uncle not ordered a portrait of his favourite to be painted?' the man asked next, his mind seeking flaws in his exciting scheme. 'Maybe a miniature?'

Peter was looking at the man in astonishment.

'You ask odd questions, Master Parker,' he said petulantly. 'I know of no portrait . . . miniature or otherwise.'

Parker laughed then, a quick sharp laugh of pleasure. He leaned across the table and patted the boy's shoulder affectionately.

'You give excellent replies, Peter,' he said. 'I think you will not be disappointed when I explain why I ask such questions.' He watched the boy with a greedy expression in his eyes, then pushed his chair back. 'But it is time you were home, Master Peter,' he said. 'You had best not finish that wine.'

'I have drunk more before now, sir,' Peter said stiffly, sitting more erect.

'Of that I am sure,' the other agreed. 'But I have travelled a long distance today and am ready for bed.' He smiled at the boy. 'And I have to think of something that has occurred to me. Something, Peter, that could carry you to the fortune you seek.'

Peter's eyes widened and he leaned forward eagerly.

'What have you in mind, sir?' he asked excitedly. 'I will do anything to get away from this place and to make my fortune. I hate being poor.'

'It means boldness,' the man said softly, with a cautious glance round. 'But come, boy, we'll talk more tomorrow. I have to think this out carefully, for the scheme is still new and I must be sure it can be accomplished.'

He rose and Peter had to get up, swaying as he did so. Parker took his arm and guided him from the inn and on to the street, collecting their hats on the way.

'I'll walk part of the way with you, Peter,' the man said.

'When will you tell me of this scheme you have?' Peter pleaded. 'I feel you are my friend, Master Parker, and I will do anything you wish, if it leads to fortune.'

'I believe you,' the man said approvingly. 'You are no priggish young oaf like your cousin. But enough for tonight, Peter. You will sup with me again tomorrow and I will have the matter decided . . . and do not mention this to anyone.'

'Be sure of that,' the boy answered.

They walked from the inn and past the dark bulk of the Cathedral, to the street beyond it where Lawyer Burdell's modest home was. Peter was talking most of the time, boasting of what he could do and how he excelled in school work, while Matt thought only of sport and fighting. The man hardly listened, his mind occupied with his tremendous scheme. He could see how everything could be arranged: to get this boy away from Exeter, and have him travel to Bristol with Matt and the clerk, would be simple enough, unless the lawyer had other plans for his son. Getting rid of Matt would be as easy, once he was in Bristol. He must get back to the inn and write a letter, to settle one matter. There was time for a reply to come back if he sent the letter by a special messenger, and the expense was worth while. The man smiled thinly as he walked beside Peter, gripping the boy's arm to save him from stumbling into a hole. The young fool was still babbling about himself: he would do anything to get away from his poverty-stricken home—anything, and Daniel Parker was his only true friend. If his greed and envy were enough to give him the courage to play his part, all would be well, Parker told himself. There were the makings of a true rogue in the boy, and probably his jealously would spur him to anything.

'We are there, Peter,' the man said softly, peering into the night and recognizing the boy's home. 'Do not forget. . . . You sup with me tomorrow at six o'clock . . . and you tell no one of our talk tonight. You will not be sorry, Peter.'

'I have no confidants,' the boy assured him thickly. 'I'll do anything you wish, Master Parker.'

Parker let him go, watching as the boy walked unsteadily towards the small house, then the man chuckled and turned away. His mind was working fast, probing into his scheme and seeing everything happen as he planned. Peter, the vain fool, would be easy to handle, but there were still questions to ask, to make sure that Colonel Tuke would not discover the trick being played on him. One of the boys might have scars or marks on his body that had been described by letter. Did the uncle know of Matt's love for games and rough company? Peter would know the answer to that, for he had written the letters in Matt's name. Did Colonel Tuke know Peter had written these letters, for this was the whole beautiful point of the deception? The clerk laughed softly as he hurried along the uneven street. He could see the arrival in Virginia, and Colonel Tuke greeting his nephew—a nephew he would believe to be Matthew Tuke. But Matt would be elsewhere, far south of Virginia and in another colony, the island of Barbados; sold for twelve years as a servant, a slave to some planter. Parker knew exactly how this could be accomplished, knew of a ship and her captain now in Bristol who would help in this scheme. And that done, Daniel Parker would be on his way to fortune. He would be in Virginia with the heir to great wealth, waiting only for the day when Colonel Tuke was dead and the supposed Matthew Tuke would have to share his inheritance. And if this took ten years it did not matter. Peter, pretending to be his cousin, would ask his uncle to employ the clerk, and there would be enough smaller pickings for deft hands while they awaited the final *coup*. Parker was smiling as he entered the inn and demanded paper and a pen. He asked for someone who would carry an urgent message to Bristol and was told this could be arranged. He went to his room to write the letter.

2

THE COMING OF JACKO

The seven days which followed Parker's arrival in Exeter with the letter summoning Matt Tuke to Virginia were both exciting and saddening for the boy. That he was finished with school and was setting out on a great adventure thrilled and delighted him, but as the days passed and the time for departure came near, Matt began to realize that he was leaving people and places which he might never see again. Virginia was across the ocean, almost out of the world, and he had never been far from Exeter since he was brought to his uncle's home. The city, with its steep streets rising from the river, where he had fished so often and where every pool and ripple had challenged his skill, the stooped old timbered houses, the huge spired Cathedral, and the old canal where the ships and quays made exciting playgrounds, suddenly became cosy and friendly. His uncle's house, even his own bed in a corner of the attic, seemed a safe little refuge, and there were so many possessions he must leave behind.

Leaving his aunt, for ever it seemed, was terrible, and there were dozens of others who must be left behind. Matt was a friendly boy, with no thoughts that his friendship should be confined to one sort of people. He had friends among the old sailors who gathered together on the quay to watch the ships and recount their adventures, and he liked an elderly parson he had met while fishing, who was delighted to pass on to this eager-eyed boy the accumulated water-lore of sixty years, and who had given Matt the greenheart rod that was one of his most prized possessions. The boy had dozens of friends among the apprentices of the city, and among the farmers outside it, who admired his boldness and skill with a horse. Matt liked to do things, rather than to look or think, and his companions were those who shared his tastes. He was not, he knew, clever, like his cousin, and was rather relieved to know this, but he was seldom bored or unhappy. And all he knew and did was inside Exeter. He would be lost outside the city. From what the man Parker said, his life in Virginia would be frighteningly different; now when Matt saw some rich person in the street he watched worriedly. He was not sure he wanted to live in a huge house with dozens of servants, or have to wear such grand clothes.

He gave away most of his possessions, his fishing-rod, his curved cricket bat, the model of a ship he had made under the eye of an old mariner, a bag of marbles and other treasures. Parting with his horse, a young black mare, was a terrible wrench and his last ride on her a distressing experience. He had offered the mare to his uncle, but the man preferred his own more sedate animal. Matt then offered her to Peter, and was surprised when his cousin refused the gift, and hurt by the way it was refused. Peter even sniffed and looked scornful.

'I will have no use for your horse,' he said haughtily. 'I may be leaving home as soon as you.'

Matt was startled, and greatly interested.

'Are you, Peter?' he exclaimed. 'Where are you going? Is your father sending you to London?'

But Peter could not meet the other's eager look. He turned away, his cheeks flushed and his eyes evasive.

'You will find out soon enough,' he said quickly. 'It is not yet decided.' He glanced out of the window, then exclaimed, 'Here is Master Parker. I have to talk to him.'

Then he was gone, leaving Matt bewildered by the rebuff. He hurried to his aunt, bursting into the room where she sat with two girls, sewing busily.

'Aunt Janet,' he cried, 'Peter says he is also leaving home. But he will not tell me where he goes.'

His aunt told him, and the boy could see she was worried. Peter was to be Master Parker's assistant on the *Speedwell*. The clerk had written to Captain Howell, suggesting that the boy be engaged and a reply was expected soon. Lawyer Burdell was willing for his son to go, hoping that when the ship arrived in Virginia, Colonel Tuke would invite Peter to stay there and give him a position. Matt heard the news with delight.

'That will be wonderful, Aunt Janet,' he exclaimed. 'Why don't you like this plan?'

'I wish it were someone other than Master Parker,' the woman confessed. 'I dislike and distrust the man, dearest. He has a manner of looking at you that disturbs me, and I am sure he is a bad influence on Peter. Peter has become strange in his manner since this man arrived. He avoids me, and will not say what he and Parker talk of; he is always with him.'

Matt laughed. He had hardly considered the ship's clerk, except as the means of going to Virginia. From where he stood, the boy saw his cousin and Parker walking in the cottage garden, the clerk talking earnestly and Peter listening with his head lowered.

'I must go and tell Peter how exciting this news is,' the boy cried. 'He will be company for me on the ship.'

He hurried out of the cottage to where the clerk and Peter had stopped. Parker saw him and whispered a warning to his companion. Matt was smiling a wide, delighted smile as he came up.

'Why did you not tell me, Peter?' he cried. 'It is wonderful news. When we reach Virginia I shall tell Uncle Franklyn that he is to take you ashore. We will learn to manage the plantation together. I will learn to grow tobacco and you will do the accounts. You are better fitted for a desk than I am.' He stood beaming on his cousin, waiting for the other to respond as happily. Instead Peter glanced quickly at the ship's clerk, and it was the man who replied.

'I am sure your cousin is grateful for your patronage, Master Tuke,' he said softly, 'but he is well fitted to achieve his own fortune.'

Matt gasped, astounded by the rebuff, his face reddening.

'Why, Master Parker,' he retorted hotly, 'is my cousin not able to speak for himself?'

'There is no need to be rude to this gentleman,' Peter cried indignantly. 'It is he who offers me this opportunity and I am grateful. My uncle sent *me* no invitation.'

Matt blushed, feeling suddenly guilty.

'It is because I have no parents, Peter,' he said apologetically. 'When he meets you and discovers you are far cleverer than I am, he will wish to help you also.' The boy paused then to grin widely, his annoyance gone. 'And we will have fun on the voyage, Peter,' he went on eagerly. 'It will be more enjoyable with another boy there.'

'Peter will be my assistant, Master Tuke,' Parker interrupted. 'You will be Captain Howell's guest. It is unlikely you will see much of each other.'

'What nonsense you talk, sir,' Matt retorted, his anger flaring again. He glowered at the man, then looked at his cousin, to be shocked by Peter's expression. 'Why, Peter!' he cried. 'Have I offended you? You look as though you dislike me.'

The other boy looked down quickly, then laughed as though impatient.

'We quarrel over what might not happen,' he said evasively. 'We have not yet had word from Captain Howell and he might not agree to Master Parker's suggestion.' He turned to the man. 'Shall we continue our walk, sir?' he asked. 'I am sure Matt has other matters to attend to.'

Matt watched them walk away, hurt and bewildered by his cousin's rudeness. He returned to his aunt, to tell her that he shared her dislike of the clerk.

'But I hope Captain Howell will allow Peter to join the ship,' he said, 'and I will get Uncle Franklyn to offer him a position.'

His aunt looked at him tenderly, then kissed the boy's cheek.

'You are too generous, Matt,' she said. 'I wish Peter was like you.'

'He isn't bad, really,' the boy answered. 'It is just that he dislikes Exeter and being without fortune. When he finds Uncle Franklyn welcoming him he will be happier.' The boy smiled at his aunt. 'And we will send for you, Aunt Janet,' he said, 'to come and take care of us both.'

The woman blinked her tears away, then became suddenly energetic and bustling.

'Enough of this babbling,' she exclaimed. 'Take your coat off and let us see if this shirt fits.'

Matt grinned, for once obeying her without protest, though so much fitting of new clothes bored him terribly.

'I will give half these things to Peter,' he threatened. 'He enjoys new clothes more than I do.'

And indeed Peter was watching the progress of Matt's wardrobe with more interest than his cousin suspected, and taking little interest in his own simple outfit that his mother began preparing when Parker said he had received a letter from Captain

Howell, approving Peter's appointment as the clerk's assistant. This deciding of his future seemed to make Peter more nervous than happy, and in the few days before he left home he was either foolishly boastful of how he would make his fortune, or he was being watchful of every word he spoke. He avoided his cousin and his mother, seeming to spend all his free hours with Parker, and Mrs Burdell became more and more worried. When she asked the boy why he did not stay at home more in his last few days with his family, Peter evaded her eyes.

'I am learning what my duties are to be, Mother,' he answered, trying to look composed. 'There is much to know.'

His mother wondered how true this was, but could not protest. Peter had always disliked being questioned, had always been a secretive boy, and she had long since given up trying to win his confidence or affection. She had given Matt the love Peter repulsed, and now, in a way, she was almost glad her son was leaving home. If her brother kept the boy in Virginia, with opportunities to advance himself, he would be less discontented, less envious of his cousin. If he remained in Exeter he would become like his father, soured by failure. She set herself to make the boy's outfit as good as their poverty allowed, surprised to find Peter little interested in new clothes. Usually he fussed and complained when she was making his garments, but now he took no notice of what she made or bought.

The wardrobes for both boys were completed and packed, and they were ready to leave for Bristol ten days after Parker had arrived in Exeter. They were to travel in what Matt considered great state, for a carriage was needed for Matt's two leather trunks and Peter's more modest outfit. Parker said the ordinary carrier was too slow, for Captain Howell had said in his letter that he hoped to sail in a fortnight's time, but wished his clerk and the boys to be aboard before then in case he got the ship away sooner. Expense, the clerk declared in his grandest manner, was not so important as speed, and he hired a post-chaise with a postilion. Matt swore he would travel in no such lurching discomfort, but would ride the horse Parker had hired in Bristol and which had to be returned. The clerk and Peter could have the carriage, Matt would ride—an arrangement that suited everyone.

On the morning of departure, when the luggage had been strapped securely behind the post-chaise, Matt waited until his cousin had said good-bye to his parents and had climbed into the carriage with Parker, before saying his own good-byes. He heard Parker order the postilion to leave but did not hasten his farewell. He would easily overtake the others. He shook hands with his uncle, then kissed his aunt, suddenly hating the thought of leaving Exeter. His aunt kissed him, then pushed him away gently.

'I have this for you, dearest Matt,' she said, handing him a small leather purse that she had made. 'I am afraid it is not money, but it is something I think more precious.'

The boy opened the purse, to find a medallion inside. He took it out, finding it was silver and engraved with the portrait of a saint.

'Your Uncle Franklyn gave that to me when he left England,' his aunt told him. 'It was our father's. I would like you to have it, Matt.'

He thanked her, replacing the medallion and slipping the purse into a pocket of his long riding-coat.

'I will show it to Uncle Franklyn when I see him,' he promised. 'And now, good-bye, dearest Aunt Janet. Don't be too sad, for we will send for you one day.'

They embraced again, then Matt mounted his horse. his aunt watching him proudly as he looked down.

'It is St. Anthony, dear,' she told him, 'and he will always find anything you lose.'

The boy laughed.

'Oh, the medallion!' he exclaimed. 'I will remember to ask him.'

Then he urged his horse forward, knowing he would cry if he stayed longer. He turned, to lift and wave his hat, then dug spurs into the horse's sides and was gone. The woman hurried into the house, to let the tears she had held back flow. The house seemed very empty and cold now Matt had gone.

The boy himself had wiped away tears before he overtook the post-chaise, and now he thought of the journey ahead and was happier. He called to his cousin, then rode past the carriage and ahead of it, gazing round the countryside at the familiar fields and wondering when he would see them again. But his sadness did not last long, the freshness of this autumn morning making him feel the world had opened for him. He turned to look back at the post-chaise, lurching and bumping over the uneven road surface, wheels jolting into ruts. The roads of England made travelling by wheeled vehicle uncomfortable in the eighteenth century and Matt was glad he had insisted on riding. He sat up in his saddle, proud of the two pistols he carried in his saddle-holsters and hoping they might encounter a highwayman who would get a surprise.

The travellers covered only twenty miles that day, for the road was too bad for faster movement. Matt lengthened the distance by chasing a fox he sighted in a field, but the streaking brown animal dived into a copse where the boy could not follow. He laughed, shouting good luck to the fox, then came back to join the post-chaise. He rode beside it for a time, trying to talk to his cousin, but Peter was scarcely civil. Hurt by his cousin's rudeness and disliking Parker more for the mocking smile he gave as Peter repelled Matt's friendliness, the boy rode ahead of the post-chaise again, feeling rather lonely and unwanted. He could only believe that Peter was still jealous of his being Uncle Franklyn's heir, and he wished his cousin were not like this. He would gladly share any good fortune he had.

He received the same lack of friendliness at the inn where they lodged that night, Peter seeming to prefer the clerk's company. Matt found some stable lads to talk to, asking them about the road ahead, if there were highwaymen about. He was told of one, a dangerous robber named Captain Parsons, who had stopped several coaches. It was believed that someone in Taunton carried news of rich travellers to the highwayman, someone who watched for suitable victims arriving at the inns, discovering when they would be leaving the town. Captain Parsons could then plan the hold-up, keeping out of sight until the chosen victim appeared.

'There's lads do that sort of roguery,' a stableman told Matt. 'We had one young gallows here last week, always about when travellers arrived. We drove him out of the village and I'll swear 'tis him tips off Cap'n Parsons.'

'You had better describe this young wretch to me,' Matt said, 'and if he is at our inn at Taunton I'll see he warns no one of our coming.'

'Ye'll not mistake him,' the man answered, 'for he looks a regular Adam-tiler, a pickpocket and thief. City cove, I fancy, by his language, and a lad as lusty as you could pick him up wi' one hand. But a reg'lar bludger, clawin' and kickin' when we catches him and flings him into the pond. Be watchful, young sir, if ye do come on him.'

So Matt kept his eyes alert when he rode into the wide streets of Taunton the next evening. But he saw no one to fit the stableman's somewhat colourful description. The town's innkeepers were allowing no beggars or suspicious-looking characters near their doors, so that the only satisfaction Matt had from what he had learned was in seeing the frightened expression on Peter's face when he was told a highwayman was working near the town. Parker, too, disliked the news and made a great show of preparing his pistols before the post-chaise set out again the next morning. Matt examined his own weapons, hoping they might meet the robber and break the monotony of the journey. He had his excitement before the day's journey was properly begun, for as he rode ahead of the post-chaise into Taunton's market-place he found a large crowd there, everyone evidently excited. Many of them carried cudgels, or staves, and were brandishing these as they laughed and called to each other. It seemed as though something was afoot and Matt called to a man, asking what was doing.

'Why, sir,' the man answered, grinning his delight, 'we're to whip a rogue out of the town. A young gallows who's suspected of working wi' Cap'n Parsons. If we was sure 'tis he who carries word to that robber we'd hang him up, but 'tis just suspicion.'

'Then you have no right to whip him,' Matt protested. He had seen rogues whipped through Exeter, the victims, with their wrists tied together, dragged behind a cart, while anyone who fancied the sport wielded cudgel, stick or strap. These were sights the kindly Matt would sooner not have seen, and now he tried to ease his horse out of the crowd and to get away. He saw the post-chaise had stopped and Peter and Parker were standing up in it, to look over the heads of the crowd. Matt sang out, warning his companions of what was to happen, but Peter laughed at his cousin and said they must wait and see the sport. There was a tremendous shouting and screaming all round Matt. He swung his horse round to find that the crowd had parted to make a lane, and then he saw the victim of this whipping. This unfortunate was not bound, nor being dragged behind a cart, but allowed to dodge as many of the blows being rained on him as he could. Matt cried out in horror, for the leaping, dodging figure looked like a child. Men were laughing and lunging with their weapons, blows coming at the small figure mercilessly. It was a boy, Matt could see, black hair tangled over his face as he bent and dodged, his feet bare and his clothes already half torn from him. A blow from a thick staff struck him, and the boy stumbled and fell to his knees, to leap up again almost at once with thin arms shooting out and fingers grasping the staff. Its owner was taken by surprise and now the victim had a weapon. He stood in the cleared space, inside a ring of howling people, swinging the staff and screaming defiantly at his tormentors. But his resistance could not last. Stones were being flung, cudgels beating at the boy, and he was being driven back. Matt could watch this torment no longer. He yelled at the top of his voice and drove his horse at those in front of him. They leapt away, Matt's short whip hastening their movements, then he was beside the raggedly clothed boy.

'Up!' Matt shouted. 'Behind me!'

That the boy he was rescuing was quick-witted as well as agile showed in the speed with which he accepted the invitation. He cast his staff at the crowd, gripped the arm Matt offered and swung, half-lifted by his rescuer, on to the horse's rump, where he grasped at Matt's coat and hauled himself forward as the horse leaped to Matt's spurs. It had all been quickly done, the crowd, startled by the unexpected rescue, parting as the horse came at them. Matt yelled, hearing the boy scream shrilly at his neck, then they were clear of the crowd and away. There were yells and shouting behind them, but no other horsemen were in the market-place that morning and no one pursued the fugitives. Matt laughed as he saw he had won clear and he heard the boy behind him laugh with him. He eased the horse's pace, turning in the saddle to look into a small, thin, and grimy face, a grinning mouth exposing yellowed teeth and dark eyes that showed no trace of fear, but rather glowed with excitement and jubilation.

'Thanks, mate,' the rescued boy said in an odd-sounding, throaty whisper, 'you're a gent . . . a reg'lar prince. They had me for a drubbing there.'

The boy seemed little affected by his beating, and Matt admired the cheeky courage. He laughed.

'They might yet,' he said. 'D'ye know this town? I'm seeking the Bristol road.'

'Yer on it, cully,' the other told him. 'Foller yer nose.'

Matt lifted the horse to a smarter pace again, planning to get clear of Taunton before waiting for the post-chaise. He would drop his passenger outside the town, for Matt had already guessed that this was the lad he had been warned about, the highwayman's scout. But that did not justify the thrashing he would have got, the maiming blows from heavy staves and cudgels. The young rogue seemed no more than a child, though that would bring him little mercy if he was caught again.

With the town a mile behind him, Matt stopped the horse and turned to his passenger again.

'This will serve for you,' he said, 'and I'd keep going as fast as you can go. Ye'll be posted right to Bristol and will be of little use to Captain Parsons now.'

The lad was already sliding to the ground, and he stood there, a sad-looking figure in his stained breeches and ripped coat, dark eyes suddenly watchful. Matt laughed.

'I was warned of you,' he said good-naturedly, 'so tell no fibs.'

The boy on the road grinned then, his eyes twinkling. 'You're no gull, chum,' he said flatteringly. 'Smart as paint, I can see.'

'And that will take you nowhere,' Matt retorted. 'I'm no country hick for your thieves' tricks. Off with you, before my friends come, for they are less good-natured than I am!'

The boy's eyes gleamed with admiration and then he winked, closing one eye slowly as though they had shared a joke.

'The name's Jacko,' he said in his hoarse whisper. 'And if anyone comes at you on the road tip that to them. You'll ride safe, chum.'

He winked again, smiling up at Matt, then spun on his bare feet and was gone, running along the edge of the road. Matt watched the slight figure, glad he had rescued the boy and liking the courage in the dark eyes. He grinned suddenly. Parker and Peter would be furious.

As they were, when the post-chaise arrived and Matt rode to the

vehicle. Peter began at once to scream at his cousin for a fool. Parker smiled thinly.

'They'll have you for a rogue, too,' he warned. 'It were a foolish trick.'

But Matt laughed merrily. He had enjoyed the adventure and now he was pleased at having annoyed his unsociable companions. He went ahead of the carriage, whistling contentedly, and thinking of the boy he had saved. Jacko! The word came easily and like a friendly hail, and Matt hoped Captain Parsons would appear so he could see the effect of the name. But no highwayman bothered the travellers. They passed coaches and carts, horsemen, and people on foot, Matt giving each a friendly salute, his eyes scanning ahead and on either side of the road for that thin, hungry-looking boy. But Jacko had either dodged far off the road or had run swifter than Matt and his companions travelled. Matt did not see the boy until the next morning, and when he did Jacko was not walking. He was clinging to the luggage straps, half under the post-chaise, grinning up at Matt when his rescuer dropped behind the carriage after leaving the inn where he and his companions had lodged. Matt looked down, wanting to laugh, then realized that the other boy would be shaken from his uncomfortable and precarious perch.

'You'll not hang there long, Jacko,' he greeted.

The other boy let his feet drop to the ground, walking himself upright and letting go the leather straps he had clung to. He came beside the horse, looking up cheekily.

'Why then, chum,' he said throatily, 'I'll ride with you. I'm for Bristol to be yer servant, mate.'

Matt laughed.

'And if I won't have ye, Jacko?' he demanded.

'Why,' the boy retorted, 'I come just the same. I've cottoned to yer, chum, and I'm a useful cove to have around.'

'You're saucy enough,' Matt said, amused by the boy's manner and words, 'but ye'll be better company than those I'm with. Come aboard as far as Bristol, for you are no weight for the horse.

He stopped and gave the ragamuffin an arm, lifting as the boy swung up behind him. Matt chuckled as he kneed the horse ahead again. He was waiting to see Peter's face when they stopped to rest the horses and themselves, and decided to keep behind the carriage until then. Behind him, the boy whispered suddenly.

'Mate,' he said, 'who's the coves with you?'

'My cousin,' Matt told him, 'and Master Parker, captain's clerk aboard the ship *Speedwell* that will carry me to Virginia.'

Jacko whistled softly.

'Virginia, eh, chum?' he said softly. He was silent for a few moments, then came tighter against Matt, whispering hoarsely. 'Watch 'em, mate,' he said. 'They're working on some trick. . . . Gulling you, chum.'

Matt turned in the saddle to see Jacko's face, and the boy winked slyly.

'I heard enough, chum,' he said warningly, 'an' they don't like you.'

Matt shrugged his shoulders, looking ahead again.

'They can do nothing to me, Jacko,' he said confidently. 'We go straight to Captain Howell in Bristol and he'll see to it I come to no harm if such is intended, which I doubt.'

Jacko did not reply, but his dark eyes narrowed. This young fellow was a simpleton, a greenhorn who didn't know a rogue from a horse's hoof. Jacko did. He had lived with rogues and thieves all his life, and he'd seen the faces of Matt's companions. A pair of gallow-seeds if he'd ever known any. He'd spoil their game if it touched this young fellow. Not many smart young gentlemen would have done what he had done in Taunton, coming riding down on the mob like a troop of horses, to save someone he'd never seen before. Jacko had experienced little kindness in his life, known only abuse and blows. He would pay back what he owed to his rescuer.

3

THE SPIRITER

Matt had expected his travelling companions to be shocke
when they saw Jacko and he was not disappointed. When at noo
the post-chaise drew off the road and on to a grass verge beside
little stream where the horses could drink, Peter and the cler
descended to stretch their legs and ease their muscles after th
uncomfortable ride. They saw the ragamuffin behind Matt an
Peter gasped in horror.

' 'Tis the brat from Taunton,' he exclaimed. 'Are ye mad, cousin?'

Matt grinned. After having suffered Peter's ill manners these past two days he was delighted to have done something to annoy him.

'You make a sad error, Peter,' he said, his eyes twinkling. 'This lad is my servant. Least, he says he is and I'll allow he is a determined character.'

'He is a highwayman's scrub,' Peter retorted, 'and will not travel with us. We'll hand him over to the magistrate at the next village.'

'Why, cousin,' Matt protested, 'then I must stay behind also and protect him. Captain Howell will not like that.'

Peter was furious. He turned to Parker indignantly.

'Master Parker,' he cried, 'you must stop this nonsense. We will all be robbed if this thieves' brat is allowed to travel with us.'

Matt's smile disappeared and he frowned.

'Master Parker will mind his own affairs,' he said coldly.

To Peter's annoyance and Matt's surprise the clerk made a little submissive bow, then cast a warning glance at Peter.

'Peter is apprehensive,' he said meekly. 'And I am sure he need not be. The lad seems harmless enough and if Master Tuke wishes to engage a servant, who is to deny him?'

Peter had caught the warning and now he turned away, glowering. Matt laughed.

'Down, Jacko,' he ordered. 'I'd have you more presentable and sweeter to the nose than you are. There's a stream where you can wash and I'll find you something from my chest.'

Peter cried out in alarm, swinging round and glaring angrily.

'That you will not do, Matt,' he cried.

Again Parker sent a warning glance at the boy and Peter flushed.

'Your clothes are hardly suitable for a servant, Master Tuke,' the man said smoothly. 'Perhaps Peter has something he can give, and you could repay him later with something of yours.'

'Maybe that would be better,' Matt agreed. 'Jacko in silk and lace would perhaps outshine his master. You do this, Peter, and you have the choice of my beautiful garments.'

Jacko had slipped to the ground, his eyes watchful, probing at Parker suspiciously.

'Off with you, to the stream,' Matt told him, 'while Peter gets something for you to wear. . . . And strip to the buff, Jacko. I fear it has been some time since you took a bath.'

The boy grinned up at him, then swung away and made for the stream. Matt came down from his horse, letting it crop at the grass while he and Parker unstrapped Peter's small trunk.

'Come here, Peter,' Matt called, 'and choose what we are to have.'

His cousin came forward sulkily, opening the trunk and turning over the neatly packed garments. He thrust a pair of grey cloth breeches, a coat, shirt and worsted stockings at Matt, scarcely looking at what he chose.

'He'll need shoes,' Matt suggested gratefully, 'if you have these to spare.'

He was given a pair of strongly made shoes and he carried the bundle to where Jacko had stripped and was scouring his thin body with river sand and water, concealed from the road by some bushes. Matt tossed the clothes on top of the bushes, seeing Jacko's now strangely pale face through the leaves, the dark eyes gleaming with excitement.

'Mate,' the boy whispered throatily, 'they're brewing a dish for you. Flamming you. Parker's a lurcher, chum, and got that cousin of yours hopping to his tune. What they up to, chum?'

Matt laughed, still rather proud of having had his own way over Jacko and of the way in which he had put Parker in his place.

'They cannot harm me,' he said scornfully. 'We'll be in Bristol tomorrow and with Captain Howell. Get into these duds, Jacko then come and eat bread and cheese before we ride on.'

The other boy sniffed, unconvinced by Matt's words and determined to watch Parker, and not to leave his champion's side until they had found this Captain Howell. Then Jacko gave himself up to the excitement and delight of putting on whole and clean clothing for the first time in his life. His thin cheeks were flushed, his large mouth spread in a grin and his eyes glowing with pride when he looked down at himself. The clothes were somewhat roomy for the thin, half-starved body, scoured until it felt like a pea inside a too-large pod, but Jacko knew himself a handsome figure as he stepped out from the bushes and made for the coach, strutting his pride. Matt grinned at him as he came up, then handed him a large piece of bread and a wedge of cheese. Parker eyed the boy shrewdly, a little smile on his lips, but Peter did not even deign to look. His ears still burned from what the clerk had said when Matt had gone with the clothes. Peter had started to complain that Parker had not insisted that the dirty ragamuffin be sent away, and the man had turned on him, his eyes contemptuous and his voice harsh.

'Numskull!' the clerk had spat. 'Don't ye see that he has to come with us? D'ye want that sewer rat following us to Bristol an' knowing who's who between you and your cousin? We have to keep him with us or he'd spoil the game.'

'He is going to Bristol,' Peter protested, flushing at Parker's tone.

'Aye,' the man agreed vindictively, 'and he'll go where your precious cousin is going. He's only skin and bone, but they'll find some use for him in Barbados . . . if 'tis only to strip off what flesh is there.'

The man's eyes gleamed with cruelty and Peter shivered, afraid for the moment. Parker sneered at him.

'So keep your tongue on a stopper,' he warned. 'I'm getting you a fortune and I want half of it when the time comes. Ye'll hang if ye don't do as I say.'

The boy turned away, pale with fear, not daring to speak. He saw his small trunk, now back on top of Matt's larger one, and it reminded him of how unjustly he had been treated in life.

'Aye,' he said suddenly and vindictively. 'You are right, Master Parker. I'll watch what I say.'

'Ye had better,' the man said grimly, then hissed a warning as he saw Matt strolling back to the road. The boy was smiling, thinking of Jacko's warning and amused by it.

'When do we reach Bristol, Master Parker?' he asked as he came near the man. 'Surely we should not be far away by this time tomorrow?'

The man smiled, shaking his head.

'I doubt it, sir,' he said. 'Nearer dusk, I'd say.'

'And we go straight aboard the *Speedwell*?' Matt inquired. 'Or has Captain Howell a house in Bristol?'

Again the man shook his head.

'He lodges at an inn,' he answered. 'We should find him there.'

It was indeed coming dark before the travellers reached Bristol, crossing the bridge over the River Frome as the stall-keepers were setting out their lanterns. Matt had found the last hours of the journey the most interesting of all, for as the travellers approached the city the road became more and more crowded. The postilion had to shout and strike out with his crop at boys who ran alongside the horses, or thrust grimy hands into the post-chaise as they begged for coppers. Slow, lumbering carts delayed the lighter vehicle on the narrow roadway, and a fast London flyer overtook them and rattled past, sending foot travellers leaping in to the hedges. Matt, with Jacko behind him, rode behind the post-chaise to keep an eye on the baggage—for the straps would have been cut and the trunks seized and whipped away by the many rogues. The boy was excited by the noise and the sights. He had been impatient to reach the city, annoyed by what had seemed to him too leisurely a day's travel. Parker, it had almost appeared, was delaying their progress, for he had called for several stops and complained of feeling sick with the carriage jolting, demanding more rest than seemed necessary. Jacko, holding to Matt, had sniffed his suspicions, telling his companion that the clerk was playing some game, until Matt bade him stop croaking. Game or no game, Parker could do no harm now. In a few hours they would be with Captain Howell.

They clattered across the bridge, its surface a narrow, crammed gangway between rows of houses and shops. The stalls on the bridge were lighted by lanterns now, though the daylight had not yet gone. Shopkeepers stood at their doors and shelves, protecting their goods from any thieves and calling their wares. The smell of the many goods mixed thickly with the stench of the river, used as a dumping-place for the town's refuse, but it was all a new experience to Matt. He sniffed in the odour of soap, tallow, leather, dyes and animals, looking everywhere, laughing down at the beggers who tried to cling to his stirrups, hearing Jacko's throaty screams abusing them in a language they understood. Matt laughed as he listened, delighted with his companion's eloquence. He rode closer to the post-chaise as it emerged from the bridge and climbed steeply through a narrow street, having to dodge shop sign-boards showing the emblems of every sort of craft: the half-moon and wheat-sheaf of a draper, the golden boy of a jeweller, the Bible and sun of a bookseller, and dozens more dangled out from the overhung buildings and could be dangerous to the unwary horseman. Kept busy avoiding the signs and keeping close to the post-chaise, Matt did not notice they were coming away from the busier streets until Jacko tugged at his coat.

'We're leaving the city, mate. Where's this cove taking us?' the boy demanded.

Matt could see that the street they were passing through was less crowded, and that the buildings were not so crammed and had gardens. They were still climbing, and now a huge building, a church, appeared against the darkening sky.

'We'll find out,' the young fellow said, urging his horse ahead and coming alongside the carriage. Parker peered up at him from a window.

'Why do we leave the city, Master Parker?' Matt asked politely.

Parker smiled, teeth gleaming in the dusk.

'We go to the harbour, young sir,' he explained, 'to where Captain Howell lodges. He has to be near the ship.'

The explanation was plausible and Matt nodded.

'We could have been here in daylight,' he complained, 'had you not made so many delays.'

'I was unwell,' the man said meekly. 'But 'tis only a short distance now. Another half-hour will see us lodged.'

Matt let the horse drop behind the carriage, to hear Jacko's throaty whisper at his ear.

'Keep a hand near your pistol, chum,' he said warningly. 'The cully's over-civil.'

'You are too suspicious,' Matt chided. 'We are in Bristol now.'

They were passing the huge bulk of the Cathedral, the road beginning to dip downward in the long gradual slope to the riverside, to where ships were clustered at wharves where the River Frome joined the Avon. The land climbed steeply on their right, towards the heights of Clifton, the darkening countryside containing only cottages and orchards. Soon, they could see against the sky the tall masts of ships on their left hand, a cluster of warehouses, and buildings with lighted windows around them. Parker leaning from the carriage, instructing the postilion, and the man guided his horses into a narrow, foul-smelling lane and stopped to Parker's shout. Matt could see a low thatched building, its windows lighted dimly; men's voices were coming from the open doorway. Parker was getting out of the post-chaise and Matt rode closer.

'If you will kindly wait,' the clerk said, 'I will inquire if Captain Howell is in the inn.'

'And if he is not?' Matt asked.

'Then we will go to the *Speedwell*,' the other answered. 'I will be gone only a moment.'

He turned away, Matt watching him.

'I trust that rogue no farther than I could throw him,' Jacko snarled thickly. 'Keep you peepers open, chum, and your hand on your pistol. This is a thieves' hole if I've ever seen one . . . an' I have.'

Matt felt himself agreeing with the other lad, thinking that this seemed an odd place for a ship's captain to lodge. But Parker had explained that Captain Howell had to stay near his ship, and this could be so. But the boy gripped a pistol as he waited, eyes peering watchfully. Then Parker appeared, smiling ingratiatingly.

'Captain Howell is here, sir,' he said respectfully, 'and bids us go to him. He is in a parlour behind the tavern.'

Matt was relieved. He told Jacko to get down, then followed, holding his horse's reins until Peter came from the coach. A man appeared, smelling of stables.

'This fellow will see to your horse and the baggage,' Parker said smoothly.

'An' take your pistol,' Jacko whispered against Matt's neck, but the boy shook his head. He could not approach his uncle's friend with a weapon in his hand. He left the pistols where they were, in the saddle-holsters, to follow Parker as the man turned into a low doorway. A reed torch flared from a bracket at the end of a narrow passage, giving enough light for Matt to see and follow the clerk. The man opened a door at the end of the passage and stood aside for the three boys to enter, Matt going first, with Jacko close behind and Peter last. Parker followed, closing the door behind him as a man's voice sang out in thunderous greeting.

'A welcome, lad,' the voice roared, 'if ye'll say who's my old chum's nephew? You, lad? I'll swear 'tis, and no mistaking. The same cut as yer uncle . . . me old chum Colonel Tuke.'

The speaker who rose from behind a long trestle-table and offered a huge thick hand seemed like a mountain inside the low-ceilinged room. His body was tremendous, a huge stomach bulging over the table, and his shoulders stretching almost to bursting a dark blue coat of thick silk. The face that beamed on the boy fitted the body, shining like a moon in the light of two candles standing on the table, though the cheeks and jowl sagged in folds of flesh. But the eyes were merry and Matt found himself smiling at the man, even as he was startled by his uncle's choice of friends. The sailor was dressed splendidly enough for his rank, but he was far from clean. His coat and a long embroidered waistcoat were stained as though grease had dripped on them, the lace at his neck was soiled and torn, his skin shone with perspiration, and his dark brown wig needed a barber's attention and was tilted to one side, as though it had been clapped on hastily.

The man had grasped Matt's hand, smothering it with his great fist and squeezing until Matt uttered an 'Ouch'. The man laughed, a great roar of merriment that shook the beams overhead, slackening the cruel grasp. He sat down again, gripping the edge of the table and gazing at the boy delightedly.

'A lusty lad, by the length of my main yard,' the sailor roared. 'Let's see who else is here.'

His eyes, suddenly sharp and assessing, went to Jacko, now standing close against Matt and watching the huge man with keen, suspicious intensity. The man's mouth opened in a wide, amused smile.

'Who's this chit?' he demanded. 'He needs feeding.'

'This is Jacko, whom I have taken as servant, sir,' Matt explained. 'I hope he will be permitted to sail with me.'

The sailor's grin widened.

'He'll serve,' he said, 'though there's little to him. I've seen such faces in Newgate, or I'm sadly mistaken.'

'Ye'd know, Cap'n,' Jacko retorted pertly and the man stopped smiling, to glower at the boy. Then he laughed suddenly.

'Aye, lad,' he agreed, 'I've shipped many a rogue from such places. . . . Ye'll meet with some tonight, for I only wait their coming.'

Parker had come forward and was standing almost against the long table, looking at the sailor.

'Tonight, Captain Howell?' he asked, sounding mildly surprised.

The other nodded, looking up at the clerk.

'Tonight, Master Parker,' he answered, 'for the *Speedwell* is loaded and anchored in King's Road. We join her by boat as soon as this gallows-meat arrives.' He slammed a fist on the table then, looking at Matt. 'Ecod, lad . . . ye'd best eat,' he roared. 'I'd

forgot ye've been on the road. Ye'll need something stowed under your belt, for we leave here within the hour.'

'You mean we are going to the ship, sir?' Matt exclaimed.

The man nodded, his loose jowls shaking.

'That's right, lad,' he said. 'I finished my cargo this forenoon and had the ship drop down to King's Road wi' the tide. We heave up with the daylight, for the wind's fair and I lose no time.' He turned to Parker. 'You, clerk,' he shouted, 'hail that servant wench and have her bring in some cold beef and ale for them lads . . . Hullo . . . another of 'em? Who's this ye've found, Parker? Ye'll have the ship as crammed as a slaver.'

Peter had kept to the background, standing there as though wishing to conceal himself. Parker smiled apologetically.

' 'Tis the lad I wrote to you about, Captain Howell,' he explained, 'who is to be my assistant.'

The sailor peered at the boy, then nodded.

'Aye, I remember,' he said at last. 'An' you and he can go ahead of us. There's the gig alongside the wharf, wi' stores in her. You and this lad go straight to her, for we'll be enough in the other boat.'

Parker bowed respectfully.

'But Peter will require supper as well,' Matt protested.

'Let him wait,' Captain Howell retorted. 'He's clerk's runner now, and small beer. A hungry belly will make him the keener. . . . Off wi' ye, Parker.'

'Will ye have room for Master Tuke's trunks in your boat, sir?' the clerk asked. 'They are a fairish size.'

'Then you'd better have 'em in the gig,' the other answered. 'Have the steward put 'em in the best cabin.'

The clerk bowed and backed from the table, while Matt looked round, puzzled by all this haste. He saw Peter's face, pale and oddly strained-looking, the eyes staring at Matt. But Parker was already with Peter, grasping his arm and turning him towards the door. Jacko tugged at Matt's sleeve, and when the boy looked at him he nodded towards the door, clearly saying they should go with Parker and Peter. But Matt was bewildered by what had happened. He could not be so ill-mannered as to say he would leave Captain Howell, or prefer to stay with his cousin. He shook his head, then a sudden noise diverted the boy's attention. It was a clinking of metal, a shuffling sound, and a voice roared in the passage:

'Lift them, you gaolbirds . . . Move yer dirty bodies afore I prick ye with this cutlass.'

Captain Howell was rising, gazing at the doorway through which Parker and Peter were already gone, and Matt watched with him. To his amazement four men were being thrust into the room, each shackled at the wrists and ankles and secured together with a long chain. Two men carrying cutlasses came behind the prisoners, and now they ranged their charges in front of the table and stood grinning at Captain Howell. He was smiling, examining the shackled men with greedy interest. His eyes stayed on one man, as tall as himself, except that he lacked the sailor's great paunch and his cheeks and chin did not sag slackly. Instead, the face was hard and scarred, the mouth stretched derisively.

'Ye like yer bargains, Cap'n?' this man asked. 'Worth the carrying, ye'd say?'

He was answered by an equally wide grin.

'Ye'll do,' the sailor answered approvingly, 'if ye don't eat too much on the passage . . . Let's see what else we have.'

He examined the others, looking pleased as he saw a short, sturdily built Negro wearing only breeches and a torn shirt. His two other bargains were not so satisfactory, for the man frowned at a man so tall that he had to keep his head bowed to avoid the ceiling beams and thin as a rake. The fourth was middle-aged and fat, and looked frightened to death. Captain Howell snorted.

'They'd have well hanged you two,' he said brutally, 'for ye'll fetch little and are not worth the feeding.' He gestured to the armed seamen. 'Take 'em away,' he ordered. 'Stow 'em in the fore end of the boat. We'll be with ye in half an hour.'

The prisoners were prodded to the door, the scarred-faced man

turning to grin at Matt and then to spit in front of the table where
Captain Howell was sitting once more. The sailor chuckled,
rubbing his great hands together.

'They'll cure him where he is going,' he said in a tone of
satisfaction.' 'I've seen them like that before.'

'But, sir,' Matt asked. 'Who are they? Why are they shackled?'
Captain Howell looked surprised.

'Rogues, lad,' he said, 'who've saved their necks by pleading to
be sent to the plantations. They'll serve seven, maybe twelve
years as servants and then be freed . . . if they're still alive.'

The boy was horrified. He had heard of criminals being transported to the colonies, but that the ship he was to sail in carried
such desperate men shocked him.

'And they sail with the *Speedwell*, sir?' he exclaimed.

The sailor looked amused.

'An' why not, lad?' he demanded. 'My ship is no slaver, nor
even a spiriter, but I will carry whoever is paid for, and these
rogues are profitable cargo.' He seemed to realize he was shocking
the boy and became suddenly watchful. 'But, there, boy,' he
said apologetically, 'you do not know the evil in this world. There
are dozens of ships out of Bristol who carry no other cargo. If
they are not carrying savages from Guinea, they are spiriters, and
that's a shameful trade.'

'Spiriters?' Matt asked. 'Who are they?'

'Why, bless yer innocent heart!' the man answered, shaking
his head until his wig slipped more sideways and his cheeks and
chin shook. 'Ye don't know what a spiriter is? Why, 'tis the
wretches who kidnap young children . . . girls as well as
lads . . . and take them to sell in the colonies. 'Tis dangerous for
homeless children to wander this way on a dark night, lad, or even
grown men and women. They'll be stowed aboard a vessel afore
they know where they are.'

'And this is permitted by the townspeople?' Matt asked in
disgust.

The sailor snorted.

'In Bristol, lad,' he said solemnly, 'they'd sell their grand-mothers. They've got trade an' profits for their religion in this city, Matt boy, and it matters little if it's a ton of Cornish copper or a hungry vagrant. . . . Mind ye,' and here the man seemed to be trying to find an excuse for the spiriters, ' 'tis the starved and homeless they take aboard and maybe some of them are better off on the plantations. When they've served their time, why, they are free to go and make their fortunes.'

'If they are still alive, did I hear ye say?' Jacko retorted hoarsely. 'I've heard of the plantations . . . where they slave until they drop, and then the overseer's at them with the lash. I'll warrant few live their term.'

'Maybe so, maybe so,' the man agreed. 'But this is dismal talk for a lad going to a great fortune. Let's hail that serving-wench and get aboard. 'Tis a long pull down the river and I intend to carry the ebb a long way tomorrow.'

He rose, pushing his bulk up with his arms, then going to the door to roar for the servant. A slattern came into the room, carrying wooden platters, to be followed by a man in a dirty apron who laid out a large piece of beef and sent the girl scurrying for bread and ale. It was an unappetizing meal, but both boys were hungry. Jacko tore at his food as though he had never eaten before, his dark eyes watching the sailor, and clearly still suspicious. But he could do nothing. Matt was accepting their host and the sailor was keeping him entertained with tales of his career. With the boys' hunger satisfied, the man rose and said it was time to go. He tugged a three-cornered hat on to his wig and reached to the bench beside him, to produce a large pistol that he thrust inside the top of his breeches.

'Now, me lads,' he announced, 'we'll to the boat.'

He took Matt's arm as though with affection, holding it as they passed to the dark lane. There a man was waiting, wearing a cutlass and bearing a flaring and smoking torch. He led them from the narrow lane to the wharf, and to steps leading to the water. A boat was alongside, the flare showing the four prisoners crowded at the fore end, two men ready on the rowing thwarts and two others holding cutlasses and pistols.

'In with ye, lads,' the captain ordered.

Matt and Jacko climbed into the boat, to sit aft, while the shipmaster got aboard with a surprisingly nimble movement and sat between them on the stern seat. The painter was let go and the boat pushed away from the wharf, drifting with the tide towards where the River Avon would carry it to the anchorage. Matt peered up, seeing ships alongside the wharf and hearing men's voices. Jacko, on the captain's other side, was darting uneasy glances around him. The boat drifted slowly past the moored vessels, the men shipping their oars, then lying back on them to send the boat ahead faster. The wharf was at the mouth of the Frome, and soon the boat was coming towards the wider Avon. As it passed close under the stern of the ship at the end of the wharf, Matt looked up. He could see the lofty stern, light glowing from the windows of the great cabin, and as the boy looked up he heard a man's deep and pleasant voice. Then, someone else spoke —a boy's voice, and Matt started, half rising from his seat. Another voice spoke, smoothly and respectfully, and Jacko exclaimed excitedly.

'Peter's on this ship,' Matt cried. 'I heard him.'

'Aye, mate, and Parker . . .' Jacko shouted. 'We're being gulled, chum.'

Both boys made to stand up, but a huge hand grasped Matt and dragged him down again. He shouted 'Peter! Captain Howell!' turning to beat his fists at the man who held him. He saw one of the armed sailors grasping at Jacko, heard the boy's oaths as he fought back. The boat tilted and rocked to the struggle, Matt fighting desperately. He was held by thick powerful arms, crushed against a sailor, and he kicked up. He heard a roar of anger, then something hard and hurting struck his head and he went limp. The man who held him lowered him to the boat's bottom, while near them Jacko fought the fat captain with a fury that brought oaths from those trying to subdue him. The supposed

Captain Howell was roaring for his men to lie back on their oars; someone was calling from the ship, demanding to know what was going on. The boat surged ahead, Jacko panting and abusing the sailor who had borne him down and now sat on him, threatening to tear his heart out if he didn't pipe down. The boat went ahead, into the centre of the river and away from the wharf, then was swung downstream, the oarsmen's task lightened by the ebbing tide.

In the comfortable, candle-lit great cabin of the ship *Speedwell*, the real Captain Howell turned from the open window in the stern, to frown towards a white-faced, scared-looking boy, and then glance at the man Parker.

'I could ha' sworn I heard someone shouting my name,' the ship's captain said.

Parker shrugged his narrow shoulders, his thin lips curling into a contemptuous sneer.

'Some drunken mariners, sir,' he said smoothly. 'It may be one of them has sailed with you in the past and was being impertinent.'

'Aye, maybe so,' Captain Howell agreed, then dismissed the matter from his mind. He looked towards the boy, a boy, he thought, who hardly came up to his uncle's proud description. This lad seemed nervous, even frightened, and had not the appearance of the sporting boy Colonel Tuke spoke of so often and with pride. But then, the ship's captain decided tolerantly, this is a new and strange world for the boy. He smiled sympathetically.

'All that shouting has upset ye, Matt,' he said. 'I think ye'd best get some sleep. Parker will show you to your cabin.'

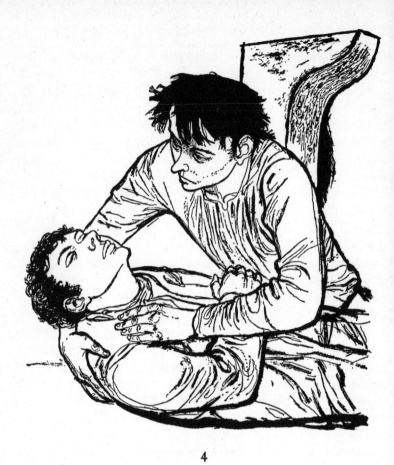

4

JACKO'S CHALLENGE

Matt was still unconscious when, two hours later, he was lifted aboard a ship anchored at the mouth of the River Avon. He moaned as a rope fastened round him under his arms tightened and he was swung upwards, but he did not know what was happening. He was carried to a hatchway and lowered down, a man following to unfasten the rope and drag the boy against a bulkhead. Jacko, abusing his captors with spitting fury, was thrust into the hatchway and on to a ladder that he almost dropped from in his haste to find Matt. He heard the other boy's thick breathing and made for him, feeling over his face and then easing him into a more comfortable position on the wooden decking. A light came, a lantern in a man's hand, and then the clank of shackles. The four prisoners came down the ladder clumsily, followed by two sailors who ordered the prisoners to sit against the ship's side, then padlocked their ankle fetters to a chain secured to the planking.

'There, mate,' one of the sailors said good-naturedly as he finished his task, 'that'll keep ye from wandering round the ship.'

The scar-faced prisoner grinned, showing broken and stained teeth, his eyes glinting in the light from the lantern.

'I'd had sooner lodged wi' that fat slob o' a captain,' he said contemptuously. 'But this'll serve for the time.'

The three other shackled men sat with their backs against the ship's side, accepting their fate. The seaman who had secured the men looked at Matt and Jacko as though doubtful.

'What about them younkers?' he asked. 'They goin' to be secured?'

'Captain Marlow didn't say,' the other seaman answered. 'One's near croaked and the other ain't more'n a runt. They can do no harm.'

The scar-faced prisoner chuckled.

'You should ha' seen that runt two hours ago, mate,' he said with relish. 'About tore yer captain's eyes out and nigh kicked his fat belly in.'

'Then he's due a lacing,' a sailor said grimly. 'I seen men keel-hauled for answering back, never mind touching, Cap'n Marlow.'

Jacko scowled at the man, dark eyes burning.

'Git out of here, ye swabs,' he spat, 'afore I do the same to you. And send down some water for my mate.'

The seamen laughed, amused by the boy's fury. They climbed out of the bare compartment, watched vindictively by Jacko. He turned to peer down at Matt, discovering the other boy's breathing was easier and his eyes were open, staring up. Then the light was gone and a cover slammed over the hatchway, leaving the prisoners in darkness.

'Are you all right, chum?' Jacko whispered throatily.

Fingers grasped his arm and Matt groaned.

'My head, Jacko,' he complained. 'It hurts.'

'You got hit wi' a pistol butt,' Jacko told him, hate in his voice. 'When ye yelled out.'

'I heard Peter,' Matt said, his voice weak and sounding bewildered. 'He was in that ship we passed, Jacko. What happened?'

The other boy made a spitting sound, expressing disgust.

'We was properly flammed,' he answered. 'That hemp-seed Parker gulled us proper; 't wasn't yer Cap'n Howell at all, mate. . . . His name's Marlow and we're aboard his ship, the *Avon Pride*.'

Matt was trying to sit up and Jacko put an arm under him, helping him to rest against the bulkhead. The boy groaned as pain shot through his skull and he raised a hand to his neck.

'Take it easy, chum,' Jacko urged. 'You got a proper wallop.'

'But why are we aboard this ship?' Matt asked weakly.

'Because that Judas Parker sold us to this Marlow,' Jacko told him. 'He tells me in the boat. . . . We're for the plantations, chum . . . sold in Barbados when we gets there.'

Matt gasped, gripping at the other boy.

'They can't do that, Jacko!' he cried. 'Why did Parker do this to us?'

'I got a good notion why,' the other answered. 'So's that lurcher, yer precious cousin, can pass off as you. I was a numps not to see Parker's game. . . . His and that prig's, yer cousin's.' The speaker heard Matt moan and slide sideways and he whispered, 'You lie back, chum . . . We got a long time to talk about this.'

'That's right, lad,' a voice said from the darkness. 'A long time. . . . Maybe twelve years if ye're lucky.'

Jacko snorted as he lowered Matt back on to the decking.

'We ain't there yet, mate,' he retorted, 'an' when we gets there we ain't so easy to hold. I'm no hobnail to be pushed around.'

A chuckle came from the darkness and Jacko grinned towards the sound. He leant over Matt, now sunk back into unconsciousness, then eased himself down against the other boy. He lay listening, hearing Matt's breathing become easier and more regular, the men across the compartment settling themselves on the planks, their chains clinking as they moved.

'Your chum all right, younker?' a voice asked.

'Sounds like he's sleeping,' Jacko answered. 'They swabs ain't brought no water like I asked.'

The man across the deck chuckled.

'You wasn't civil enough, lad,' he retorted. 'I'd hitch a stopper on that tongue of yours for a while. Ye're at sea now, lad, and this Cap'n Marlow ain't no greenhorn.'

The man laughed as he heard Jacko's scorching reply, then worked his shackled arms into a more comfortable position and closed his eyes. This lad sounded a real knock-out and would make the voyage to Barbados lively. The man grinned as he remembered how Jacko had flung himself at Marlow in the boat, tearing at his face, knocking his wig into the river and kicking at him until the fat sailor was yelling for help. They'd got the lad down, three to hold him, until he gave up struggling and started abusing them in as ripe a language as they had ever heard. Captain Marlow had threatened to throw the boy into the river if he didn't pipe down, then told him he was sorry for whoever bought him in Barbados. The prisoner began to feel as sorry for whoever did buy the boy, he'd own a tartar.

The noise of men tramping overhead, the creak and screech of a capstan being walked round, block sheaves squeaking as they took the weight of sails being raised, and the roaring abuse of the ship's captain spurning on his crew wakened the six prisoners. Matt awoke to see a thin line of daylight above him, coming through between two planks in the hatch cover and spreading to give enough light to show the boy where he was. He remembered, and made to sit up, then cried 'Ouch' and gripped his head as pain shot into it. Jacko pushed himself up, glancing round quickly, then looked at Matt anxiously.

'You all right, chum?' he demanded.

Matt nodded, grimacing, but letting his hands drop. He gazed at Jacko.

'We've been spirited, Jacko,' he said helplessly. 'Parker sold us to that fat man.'

Jacko looked relieved.

'You remember, chum?' he said. 'That's good. I thought you might be knocked for good. You looked bad last night.'

The four men were awake and sitting up, the scar-faced man grinning cheerfully.

'How's the head, lad?' he asked. 'Stopped singing a tune?'

Matt looked at the man, nodding slightly.

'Thank you, sir,' he said. 'It isn't too bad now.' He turned to Jacko. 'I've got you into a terrible mess, Jacko! You'll wish you'd never seen me.'

'I ain't worrying about that,' the other said. 'I allus wanted to have a sea voyage. Ain't never been on a ship before.'

'You'll see little of this one, Jacko,' the scar-faced man remarked. He looked round at his companions. 'How about introducing us?' he demanded. 'I'm Sam Bridger, sailor what's gone wrong.'

The man looked so cheerful and confident that Matt had to smile.

'My name is Matt Tuke,' the boy said. 'I met Jacko on the road to Bristol.'

'And you ran against this spiriter,' Bridger said, his voice inviting the boy's story.

'We were tricked,' Matt told him. 'I was to meet a captain named Howell, whose ship is the *Speedwell*, and was to sail with him for Virginia where my uncle lives.' The boy paused, upset for the moment, and Jacko ended their story.

'An' we was flammed by a pen-pusher called Parker,' he said in his throaty voice. 'He gets us took by this spiriter while he passes off Matt's cousin as him, so's he can have his uncle's plantation.' Jacko snorted his contempt. 'He ain't going to have much left when Parker's claimed his share,' he added spitefully, 'and I'll be there to laff.'

'You'll be planting tobacco and cutting sugar in Barbados, Jacko,' Bridger said grimly. 'Wi' yer back gouged wi' the cat if ye look above yer shoulder.' He turned to the three men beside him. 'Let's have your yarn, shipmates, and cheer up. You got a long soft voyage ahead, wi' no hard work and grub served like you was lords. What's your tally, nigger?'

The Negro had been watching Bridger with large admiring eyes and now he grinned, showing perfect white teeth.

'Me, master,' he said in a voice like a foghorn, 'I'm a runaway. Servant to Master Hasting in London, who buys me from Cap'n Jones, but I runs away because he whips me. I gets hungry and steals a loaf, and they goes to hang me up but they don't.'

'New York born or I'm a longshoreman, the sailor commented. 'An' you, beanpole? Wot you been? A hop-master?'

The tall painfully thin man turned a doleful face to his questioner, shaking his head.

'Adolphus Marlborough Hardcastle, sir,' he answered sadly. 'One-time clerk in Holy Orders, then scribe. I wrote a poem, sir. Fifty lines only, and without blemish. For this I was colleged, sir—in Newgate. I had insulted our gracious Queen, they said.'

Bridger listened with delight and Jacko eyed the thin man suspiciously.

'Long Tom, or I'm a ranker,' he exclaimed suddenly. 'Best queer-shover in London. I heard about you, mister.'

The man blushed and looked embarrassed.

'You keep disgraceful company, boy,' he chided, gazing at the boy sorrowfully.

Bridger leaned over, chuckling.

'Counterfeit money, eh?' he said.

'A scribe, sir,' the other insisted, 'but one must live and to live one must eat. Alas, work is involved and that leaves no time for poetry. I was forced into crime, sir, by the inequalities of this world.'

The sailor laughed, then turned to the fourth person, a small, stout, and middle-aged man with a meek expression who spoke without being questioned.

'My name is Bassett, sir, and I merely tried to poison my uncle,' he explained apologetically. 'He is eighty years of age and has had a good life, and I was his heir.'

'Ye fumbled the job, chum?' the sailor asked, grinning.

'Alas, yes, sir,' Bassett agreed. 'The chemist lied to me. He swore five grains would be ample.'

'Maybe your uncle was tough,' Bridger suggested and the other looked at him worriedly.

'It could be, sir,' he answered. 'I would have sued the chemist if I had not been sent here.'

Both Bridger and Jacko had listened to the stories with delight, but Matt gazed from man to man, amazement and horror in his face. He had never been among criminals in his life until now, and that people did what these men confessed to having done shocked the boy.

His thoughts were interrupted by the hatch into the compartment being flung open and something dropped down to land with a crash. It was a bundle of chain. Two men, villainous-looking characters with their hair drawn back and plaited, descended, one of them carrying a hammer. He grinned at the prisoners.

'You, sprig!' he announced, gazing at Jacko with a leer. 'Cap'n says you're to be fitted wi' them irons.'

Matt started up in horror.

'Leave him alone,' he commanded. 'He has done nothing to you.'

'He nigh tore out the Cap'n's eyes last night,' the man said, standing back to admire Jacko. 'An' got the makings o' a mutineer. Best have him in bilboes, Cap'n says, and here we are to fit him cosy as ye like. . . . Stay where ye are, shrimp, or I'll tap ye one with this.'

He held his hammer up and Jacko sneered.

'Got ones to fit?' he taunted.

The man laughed.

'We make 'em fit if they don't,' he said. 'Let's have 'em, Bart.'

Jacko's legs were shackled together at the ankles, some two feet of chain between the anklets. They fitted somewhat loosely, but were seemingly tight enough to satisfy the sailors. The bands were closed and fastened with soft iron bolts. Jacko then was shackled at the wrists, the chain allowing him some movement, and finally an anklet was padlocked to a lighter chain already set into the wooden bulkhead. Matt watched helplessly and sorrowfully, but Jacko appeared unconcerned. He taunted the sailors with insults as they secured him, earning himself a cuff when his abuse annoyed one man. The boy spat his contempt, then sat back, sneering.

'What about me?' Matt demanded when the seamen had finished with Jacko. 'You had better secure me also.'

One of the men shook his head.

'You got to see the Cap'n' he announced. 'He's setting ye up handsome in a cabin. Got plans for you, younker.'

'I'll have none of them, tell him,' Matt retorted. 'He is a villain and a wretch . . . a dirty spiriter.'

The sailor looked puzzled, scratching his head and eyeing the boy.

'Look ye, younker,' he said apologetically, 'I got another set o' darbies if you gets awkward. Cap'n says he's willing to treat ye right if ye behaves proper, but if ye don't ye'll be treated same as them scruff till ye come to yer senses. . . . Don't go making it rough on yerself, lad.'

'Put them on me,' Matt cried hotly. 'I want nothing from that foul creature.'

The man shrugged his shoulders, then looked at his companion.

'Seems like we got to secure this younker, too,' he said resignedly.

'You do what they says, Matt,' Bridger advised. 'Might as well lie soft, though I'll eat them chains if Marlow isn't playing some trick where he needs you.'

'He knows about Parker and yer cousin,' Jacko said, 'an' he's planning to give them the double-cross. . . . Get word to yer uncle he's being gulled, and get a reward. You do what he says, Matt.'

'That I will not,' the other boy retorted; 'I'll stay with you,

Jacko. We'll find some way of reaching Uncle Franklyn and he'll have this rogue punished with the others.'

'You're a mug, chum,' Jacko said scornfully. 'The only way to get the best of Marlow's sort is to be more cunning than them. You're too honest by far, chum.'

One of the sailors was shaking out the second set of shackles and now he told Matt to get up and take off his long riding-coat. The boy obeyed, and his wrists were shackled. He was told to sit down and when he did the sailor fastened the iron anklets and chained him to the bulkhead. Meanwhile, the second sailor was emptying the pockets of the riding-coat and Matt protested.

'Don't blame me, younker,' the man said. 'I was to see none of you had anything ye might use to make trouble. I'm going to search the other kid as well.'

They watched as the man emptied Matt's pockets, finding a bone-handled pocket-knife, a length of cord, a small volume the boy had carried for reading on the voyage, and other harmless objects. Matt remembered his aunt's gift then, and demanded that it be handed to him.

'Purse?' the sailor asked. 'I seen no purse.'

He showed what he had taken and the purse with the medallion in it was not there.

'Then one of your shipmates in the boat took it last night,' the boy said scornfully. 'It will do him little good, for it contains only a medallion.'

Jacko's pockets produced nothing, and the boy sneered as he was searched. The seamen did not touch the men prisoners, knowing they had come from gaol and would have nothing. As the men climbed out of the compartment Bridger sang out mockingly.

'Best leave that hatch cover off, mates,' he said, 'or we'll suffocate. Cap'n Marlow wants us kep' healthy for fetching a price.'

The hatch was indeed left open and Matt was relieved. He hated the thought of being closed in to the darkness again. From where he lay he could look up, seeing sails curved and swelling from their yards, watch a rope tapping against a thick mast and hear the soft creak of ropes and blocks, the distant sound of water breaking as the ship moved ahead. It was almost pleasant lying and looking up, listening to Jacko talking to Sam Bridger. The sailor and the street arab seemed to like each other, and neither was in any way oppressed by their situation. Sam was laughing, listening to Jacko as he recounted some of the stories he had heard about the counterfeiter, the man who called himself Hardcastle, but whom Bridger addressed as Beanpole. The thin man kept tut-tutting and protesting mildly as Jacko told his story. The two others, the Negro and the man who had tried to poison his uncle, listened as well, the Negro grinning and casting admiring glances at Hardcastle. Matt looked at the men, thinking how his life had changed in the past hours. He had arrived in Bristol as a lad with a rich future, and now he was chained with criminals and being carried away to be sold as a slave. He would be called an indentured servant, but slave he would be. And Barbados was far away from Virginia. He would not be allowed to write to his uncle or to complain to any authority, but would be kept on some plantation as a prisoner for twelve years. By then his uncle would have died, and Peter would be known as Matthew Tuke. His cousin's treachery and greed horrified the boy and he could have wept in his plight. He envied Jacko the scorn the other boy showed for their fate, for his companion seemed to treat the whole terrible affair as a joke.

Matt's dismal thoughts were interrupted by a man who climbed into the compartment and began unlocking the padlocks securing each prisoner to the bulkhead.

'Up with ye, ye loafers,' he ordered. 'Ye're to have an hour on deck and yer grub. Cap'n Marlow likes to keep his cattle fat for the market.'

They all climbed out of their prison, to find two armed men waiting to guard them as they came up. A wooden tub was on the deck, with a large pewter jug of ale. The tub contained a mixture of beans and salt meat cut into cubes.

'Stick yer muzzles in that,' a man ordered. 'Yer lucky to have a kindhearted cap'n.'

'What do we eat with?' Matt demanded, then saw Jacko dip his fingers into the mess and scoop up a handful.

'I'll have the cap'n's silver spoon along for ye next time, younker,' the sailor sneered, 'and meantimes ye can use what's at the end o' yer arm. It was invented afore spoons.'

The boy was disgusted, but he was also hungry. He joined his fellow captives at the tub. They emptied it, Bridger threatening to skin Hardcastle when the counterfeiter would have taken more than his share. The jug was passed round, the ale drunk, then they were all ordered to rise and walk up and down the deck. Matt looked over the ship's bulwarks, to see land on the starboard side, a sea broken only with small waves, and to feel a wind coming from almost astern.

'There's the Holmes,' Sam Bridger said, nodding towards a small island near the mainland. 'I'll tip my hat to it next time I pass.'

Matt looked aft, to see the vast bulk of Captain Marlow on the sterncastle, the man watching them. Jacko saw the captain and screamed, asking if he wanted another scratching, a piece of impertinence that earned the boy a blow from a hand palm. He snarled at the sailor, until Bridger bade him 'Stow it'. Strangely, Jacko obeyed. Their exercise over, the prisoners were taken to the hatchway and a bellow from the ship's captain ordered the cover to be secured over them. Two seamen came below to fasten the padlocks again, then the hatch was closed. Bridger grunted.

'I'm goin' to meet up wi' that slob by and by,' he said, and his eyes were no longer good-natured. 'An' he ain't going to be pleased when I do.'

'When?' Matt asked despondently. 'After you have served seven years in Barbados?'

The sailor laughed.

'I'll not stay there more'n a week,' he said grimly. 'I'll have me out of the island and sailing for New Providence afore they can

lay a lash across my back. I've been in the West Indies afore thi
and know the tricks, and have good shipmates waiting to help
me. . . .'

'What's New Providence, Sam?' Jacko asked, watching the
man keenly. ' 'Tis a pirate stronghold, isn't it?'

'Aye, lad, an' the merriest place in the Americas,' Bridger told
him. ' 'Tis where the freebooters went when they got drove out
o' Jamaica and 'tis a proper harbour for brave sailormen.'

'Ye'd be pirate then?' Jacko demanded. 'Maybe not for the
first time?'

Bridger laughed, showing his broken teeth in a fierce grin.

'An' right ye'd be, Jacko,' he said, 'and right ye are again. Get
me ashore out o' this hulk an' I'll show ye my heels.' He looked at
the boy shrewdly. 'An' you can come with me, Jacko. Ye'd make
a smart ship's boy aboard a freebooter.'

'An' Matt?' Jacko asked quickly.

Bridger looked at Matt doubtfully.

'He's a good enough lad, I'd say,' he said at last, 'but law-
abiding as a parson. Squeamish, I'd say, wi' ideas about playing
fair. But I'd take him to oblige ye, Jacko.'

'I am sure you are very kind,' Matt said stiffly, 'but I'll have no
truck with pirates.' He glowered at Jacko. 'And you won't either,
Jacko,' he declared.

'Ye'd have us slaving in Barbados for twelve years, chum?'
Jacko retorted. 'Don't be a greenhorn, mate. You and me's got to
get to Virginia and settle wi' Parker and yer prig of a cousin, an'
if Sam here'll help us get part way there, we'd be numskulls if we
don't take the chance.' The boy turned to Bridger, dark eyes
gleaming. 'But why wait for Barbados, Sam?' he demanded.
'There's a ship here, wi' a fat cargo and six of us to take her.'

Matt gasped, but said nothing. He was out of his depths in such
company as this, and Jacko had become a stranger almost. On the
road he had been a pathetic little scruff, a hounded animal, and an
amusement to his young benefactor, but now he was treating
Matt like a child who had to be protected. There was a hardness

in his eyes, a sneer in his voice, except when he spoke to Matt, that gave him kinship with Sam Bridger and the long-faced counterfeiter, Hardcastle. The two other men, the Negro and Bassett, were pathetic and unimportant, but those three, Sam Bridger, Hardcastle, and Jacko, were birds of a feather, enemies of the law-abiding, the hawks of society. Matt felt helpless and upset, finding himself lost in such company.

Sam Bridger was grinning at Jacko, admiring him.

'How, lad?' he asked, leaning forward and speaking softly. 'How to take the ship? Let's have yer plot, Jacko, for I swear there's something brewing in that cunning mind of yours.' The man sat up, examining the boy shrewdly. 'If ye have a mind that we can take the ship when we're up for exercise, 'tis no good, lad. I had my eyes open today, and that fat man-driver is no first-tripper. He's carried desperate men afore this, and we was well watched. Marlow ain't the man to take any chances, boy.'

Jacko was sneering. He winked an eye slowly.

'You take me for a greenhorn, Sam?' he asked scornfully. 'What of the night, mate? We could take the ship when they're all asleep.'

'A ship don't ever sleep, boy,' Sam told him. 'There's the watch on deck night and day . . . and how to take her wi' them irons holding us?'

Jacko grinned then, his elbows drawing back against his sides, and suddenly he was holding both arms up, free of the shackles that now lay across his legs. Matt gasped his astonishment, but Sam Bridger was smiling broadly.

'I seen a juggler do that once,' he said softly and admiringly. 'But I thought 'twas his darbies were rigged.'

' 'Tis a trick only some can do,' Jacko told him boastfully. 'If ye are born wi' the right sort of joints. I was learned how to slip irons afore I was able to walk almost.'

Bridger chuckled.

'I'd say ye was well learned other ways too,' he said admiringly. 'Can ye slip the leg bracelets as well, Jacko?'

'Aye, and easier,' the boy answered scornfully. 'Would y
have me show you?'

'There's no hurry,' Sam said, well satisfied by what he ha
seen. 'But what of us, Jacko?' he demanded. ' 'Tis not enoug
that you are free.'

'There's files aboard the ship,' the boy answered. 'I'll fin
'em.'

'How can you, Jacko?' Matt demanded, more worried tha
hopeful. 'The hatch will be guarded.'

But Jacko and Sam were watching each other and smiling

'Where are we in this ship, Sam?' Jacko asked. 'I have n
knowledge of sea affairs.'

Sam was gazing round the compartment. It was formed by th
ship's side as one wall, with wooden bulkheads as the three oth
walls, and was some twelve feet square and five feet high. Th
only entrance or opening was the small hatch and its ladder, th
only light the thin strip pressing between the hatch planks. Th
sailor examined the place slowly.

'I'd say this is the fore end of the hold, in the 'tween deck,' h
said at last, 'boarded off for this purpose. Marlow is a spirite
though he carries cargo also.'

The man hitched himself against the bulkhead to which Ma
and Jacko were chained, his hands going over the planks slowl
fingers exploring where they met. Jacko had turned to face th
bulkhead and was searching as carefully. He grinned suddenl
then put a hand behind his head, feeling inside the back of his coa
To Matt's astonishment the other boy drew a long-bladed dagg
from his coat, to push the point between two planks and twist

'You were searched, Jacko!' Matt cried and Jacko snorted h
contempt for the searchers.

'I could a' had the post-chaise stowed away and them swa
wouldn't have found it,' he said.

Sam Bridger chuckled.

'You was schooled wrong for where ye've landed, lad,' h
told Matt, then watched Jacko as the boy twisted his dagger

make a hole. He withdrew the blade and tried to peer behind the planking. 'What's there, Jacko?' the man demanded.

'Black as the ace of spades,' the boy answered.

'Likely enough, if that's the hold,' Sam answered. 'Let's see how the planks are fastened.'

They were nailed at top and bottom, and Jacko began to dig at the wood round one nail-head near the deck. He gouged out the wood, leaving the nail exposed, the others watching as he worked. Two more long iron nails had to be cleared, but Bridger told the boy not to touch them.

'There's no hurry,' he said. 'There's a month's sailing ahead and we'll let Cap'n Marlow take her as far as Hispaniola. I'm no hand wi' a quadrant and fancy navigating, though I know the Caribbean like the palm of me own hand. Lie back, lad, time enough tomorrow to finish the task.'

Jacko pushed the dagger down the back of his coat, returning it to the scabbard fastened inside his clothing. He grinned at Matt as he pushed his hands into the handcuffs again, his hands seeming to become boneless as they passed through the iron bands. Matt could see the other boy in the fading light, his eyes glowing and his satisfied smile. Jacko was thoroughly enjoying himself now. So was the scar-faced sailor, Sam Bridger. The man chuckled as he sat back against the ship's side.

'I want to see Cap'n Marlow's face when we puts that dagger of yours to his fat neck, younker,' he said with grim humour. 'An' then see the welcome we gets when we sails this prize into New Providence. Ye'll find some proper chums there, Jacko. We'll sell the cargo and go a-roving, lad. . . . That's the proper life for a younker wi' your tricks. Ye'll be a pirate captain afore ye're many years older, or I'm a Dutchman.'

Matt heard Jacko's pleased giggle and was suddenly worried.

'Jacko is coming to Virginia with me,' he said indignantly. 'You will, Jacko?'

'Why, mate,' the other boy answered good-naturedly, 'that's to be seen when the time comes. I dunno as I could learn honest ways now, for I've been brought up a thief. But I'll think on't, chum. It ain't often I've cottoned to anyone like I has to you.'

Matt saw the other boy's wide grin, then Jacko went on. 'But we haven't taken the ship yet, mate,' he said. 'Wait till we see what's behind that plank afore we start making plans.'

5

MATT IS NOT ADMIRED

Jacko did not resume his task of opening a way into th
Avon Pride's hold the next day, nor for the next four days. O
that first night of the voyage, Matt was awakened by the dec
where he lay, tilting and lifting under him and by the impact of
wave against the ship's side. He lay, listening, hearing an ominot
whistling outside the compartment, and block sheaves creaking
ropes were stretched by the weight of wind-filled sails. The *Av*

Pride sank down, jerking uneasily, then another wave struck her and she tilted over, water breaking against her and splattering on deck.

'What's happening, chum?' Jacko's voice asked, and he did not sound like the cocksure young rogue of the previous day. He sounded nervous.

'Feels like a breeze coming,' Sam Bridger answered from the darkness. 'Got a hard sound to it. I thinks we're in for a blow.'

The *Avon Pride* had been running to a fair wind all that day, with only a whisper of sound from her rigging and water muttering along her sides. Now there was a creaking as though the ship complained; sudden, sharp jerking sounds and a low growling of water. Another sea struck the ship, exploding against her, and she tilted as water poured over the deck and raced overhead, some crushing under the hatch cover and dripping into the compartment. Jacko yelped and drew his legs back, grasping at Matt's arm. A voice roared somewhere above the prisoners, then heavily booted feet ran forward and a man was yelling urgently.

'That's them poor fellers being hauled out to strip her down,' Bridger said with mock sympathy. 'We're lucky . . . lying here all snug.'

More booted feet trampled overhead and voices roared angrily. Block sheaves squealed as sails were lowered, the canvas flapping and beating like the wings of some huge bird. There was a crash, a crunching sound, and Bridger chuckled as a voice roared abuse on the men who had let a heavy yard come down too quickly. Bridger was listening to the sounds of activity with expert ears, telling the others what was happening on deck.

'Feels like the wind is come round southerly,' he said, 'and blowing up all the time. They're getting the lower yards down on deck and reefing the topsails. . . . Maybe have to get them off her, too, if the wind comes like it sounds.'

A groan came from somewhere in the compartment and Bridger peered down.

'It's you, fatty,' he said humorously. 'What's the matter, mate?'

'I'm ill,' Bassett whimpered. 'I'm going to be sick.'

'That's right,' Bridger agreed callously. 'That's what ye get for not making a proper job of yer uncle. Might have been sitting back wi' yer grog now if ye'd done the job proper.'

The man groaned and Bridger chuckled. Matt realized that Jacko had not spoken for some time and he peered down, then touched the other boy. He was lying on his side, his knees drawn up.

'Are you all right, Jacko?' Matt asked anxiously.

'I feels awful, chum,' the other boy answered weakly. 'I wish we hadn't come on this ship.'

'Didn't have any choice, did ye, younker!' Bridger said.

The *Avon Pride* lay over, then seemed to soar upward. She hung, poised on a wavetop, before tilting forward and plunging down into a trough. A wave swarmed at her, the ship's bows striking it with a force that shook the hull and set the rigging banging and rattling. Jacko cried out, sliding on the now wet deck planks, and Matt grasped at him. The man Bassett was whimpering, crying that this was his punishment for trying to poison his uncle. Sam Bridger chuckled.

'Here's a crowd of jolly pirates,' he said mockingly. 'We got to pick fine weather when we takes this ship. Old jelly-belly lying here groaning and Hardcastle ain't no better. How you feeling Matt?'

Matt was one of the lucky people who never suffered from sea-sickness, even when he had gone out with the Exmouth fishermen and been tossed through a wild night in Teign Bay. He felt chilled, and the water dripping into the compartment was swilling back and forth, soaking his breeches.

'I've never been sea-sick' he told Bridger. 'But I wish this would stop.'

'It won't, younker,' the man told him. 'We're in for a proper tossing. I hope this ship has got plenty of sea room and don't get blown on to some cliff. We're somewhere round the mouth of the Bristol Channel now and that's a bad place.'

Bridger was right about the weather. All that night and through the next day the storm increased, the sea rising until the ship was being lifted and flung with a violence that wearied the body and dazed the mind. Matt's bones ached with the discomfort and he was chilled by the water coming into the compartment. He found his riding-coat and spread it over the now helpless Jacko, holding to the smaller boy to stop him sliding across the wet planks as the ship lay over or flung herself downward into a trough. With daylight the boy looked on a scene of misery, for only he and Bridger had not succumbed to sea-sickness. The others lay huddled on their sides, sliding helplessly when the ship lay over. Bassett had kept up a moaning and sobbing for hours, until Bridger threatened to beat his head in with his shackles if he did not pipe down. Hardcastle had just curled up like a huge spider and gone to sleep, while the Negro stared glassily as he lay. Matt was worried about Jacko, for the boy had pulled the riding-coat over his head and had not moved, except for being jolted as the ship lifted to the seas, crashing down with thunderous sounds of water that poured on the deck overhead as though engulfing the *Avon Pride*. Several times, Matt drew the coat aside to look worriedly at the other boy's drawn, pale face, each time Jacko whimpering a protest and pushing feebly at Matt's hand, begging to be left to die.

Sam Bridger was treating the storm as a great joke. When sounds of activity came from the deck above and his experienced ears told him that a sail had been blown out, or something had parted, he grinned.

'Them poor sailormen,' he mocked. 'Having an awful time up there. I could weep for them . . . 'specially Captain Marlow. Sufferin' terrible 'e'll be. Up there, wet and cold, and his belly shaking like it was coming away.' Bridger tut-tutted his sympathy. 'That'll learn young Jacko,' he went on. 'He won't want to be no pirate after this.'

The hatch was kept closed on the prisoners for four days,

except for a brief moment each day when it was raised and some-
one tossed a handful of thick ship's biscuits into the compartment.
Once a villainous-looking seamen climbed down, to hand
Bridger two bottles.

'Having a wicked time up there, mate?' Bridger remarked
sympathetically, his eyes twinkling. 'You should get yourself
transported . . . It's comfortable down here.'

The sailor growled and climbed out of the compartment,
slamming the hatch cover into place. Bridger tossed a biscuit to
Matt and began gnawing at another. The bottles contained scum-
thickened water, but the boy drank gratefully. He tried to get
Jacko to eat or drink, but he groaned and tugged the coat over his
head, pleading to be left alone.

The storm eased away on its third day and Matt awoke that
morning to find the ship lifting less violently, and to see sunshine
pressed between the hatchway planks. The boy sat up, to notice
Bridger watching him and smiling widely.

'Looks like this gale is passing,' the man remarked.

The boy felt dazed, aching all over, his wet clothes sticking
to him like plasters, and he wished he could rise and walk about.
He saw the Negro was sitting up, holding a biscuit. The others
remained curled where they lay. Matt drew the coat away from
Jacko's head and two pain-filled eyes gazed up at him.

'Where are we, mate?' Jacko whispered thickly. Bridger
laughed.

'Feeling bad, younker?' he asked. 'You'll be perky as ever
tomorrow. Here, have something to eat, lad.'

He tossed a biscuit to the boy and Jacko groaned and hid under
the coat again. Bridger grinned.

'What 'e needs is a nice big slice of fat pork,' he said heartlessly.
'That'd fix him.'

'You are a brute, Sam Bridger,' Matt protested. 'Don't torment
him.'

Bridger laughed.

'He'll be saucy as ye like tomorrow,' he said. 'You see. This breeze is finished. . . . They've put canvas on her again and we're going ahead.' He looked round the water-dripping bulk-heads approvingly. 'She's a proper ship, younker,' he said. 'Came through that gale handsomely. . . . She'll make a smart pirate ship.'

Bridger was right in predicting the end of the storm. All that day the wind decreased, shifting, Bridger said, to the north-west. The ship's movements eased, and though she still rolled and tilted she did so slowly and without the violent jerking of before. More and more sails were being set, Bridger interpreting the sounds of activity from overhead. They heard a man laugh, the first cheerful sound for days, and Matt found himself being lulled into sleep again. When he awoke it was again daylight and the hatch had been opened. Warm sunshine came into the compartment as a thick beam, cleansing the air and drying the deck planks. Sam Bridger was sitting up. Hardcastle had come from his stupor and was rubbing his long gaunt face with a grimy hand. Matt turned to look at Jacko, then drew the coat away and urged the boy to sit up.

'It's fine weather now, Jacko,' he whispered.

The smaller boy pushed himself up, gazing round dazedly; his face seemed to have become smaller and his eyes larger in the past days. He pushed his tangled black hair back, blinking and licking his lips.

'Here, sprat,' Bridger said, reaching to offer a bottle, 'have some scummy water. Do ye good.'

Jacko drank thirstily, then wiped his mouth and tried to grin at Matt.

'Ye're right, chum,' he said throatily. 'I ain't going to be no pirate. I likes solid ground after this.'

'I told ye so, Matt,' Bridger remarked, chuckling. 'Nothing like a gale of wind to show what's in a lad.'

A figure shut out some of the sunlight and a man climbed into the compartment. He looked at the prisoners humorously.

'Looks like ye enjoyed yerselves down here,' he said. 'Ye're to come on deck and have something to eat.'

He unlocked the padlocks, freeing them from the bulkhead chains, and they climbed on deck. Bassett had to be prodded with a toe to make him sit up and he looked a miserable creature now. His cheeks had sagged and were covered with a dirty grey stubble of hair, his eyes stared desperately, and he seemed to have lost weight. The sailor hustled him roughly to the ladder, Bassett complaining that he was sick and wanted a surgeon.

'The only surgeon aboard here is Cap'n Marlow,' the sailor told him, 'an' he'd cure ye wi' a rope's end.'

The wooden tub with its contents of luke-warm beans and chopped pork was waiting for the prisoners, and Matt was delighted to see how hungrily Jacko ate his share. So did Hardcastle and the Negro, and only Bassett sat listlessly, not touching the food.

'Eat up, mate,' Sam Bridger advised. 'You ain't going to die yet.'

Bassett scooped up some of the food with his fingers, but he let it drop back into the tub. The man kept glancing along the deck, to where an officer stood on the quarterdeck, and Jacko noticed the glances. He moved close to Bridger and whispered, attracting Matt's attention with the note of warning in his voice. Bridger looked at the poisoner searchingly, then leant towards him.

'Don't you try it, fatty!' he said, and though his voice was low there was a threat in it that startled Matt. 'It would get ye nothing,' Bridger was saying, 'an' we'd cut yer throat afore ye got there. Keep away from Cap'n Marlow.'

Bassett cringed, staring at the other man fearfully.

'I am ill,' he protested, 'and meant only to ask for medicine.'

'Ye'll get it,' Bridger told him grimly. '—My irons on yer skull if ye make a move to attract anyone's attention.'

He sat up again, watching the other man coldly and Matt wondered what was happening. He moved close to Jacko and whispered, asking what Bridger meant.

'That dirty traitor wants to betray us,' the other boy answered balefully. 'He's been scared and wants to get aft. Sam'll kill him if he tries again.'

A seaman came from the stern, interrupting the tense and somehow frightening little scene. He looked at Matt and gestured aft.

'Cap'n wants you, younker,' he said. 'In his cabin.'

Matt was startled, then alarmed at the prospect of meeting the shipmaster again.

'I don't want to see him,' he protested quickly. 'I won't go near him.'

Sam Bridger looked amused and Jacko was watching Matt in surprise.

'See what he wants ye for, chum,' the smaller boy advised. 'Can't do no harm.'

Bridger laughed.

'Might offer ye a soft berth aft, lad,' he said.

'So he might,' Jacko exclaimed in his hoarse whisper. He leant towards Matt. 'Ye'd be handy there, chum.'

Matt flushed, knowing what Jacko was suggesting. If Captain Marlow did invite him aft he would be able to help more in taking the ship. He might even find the files that were needed to free the others.

'You'd best come aft, younker,' the sailor advised. 'Cap'n Marlow don't like to be crossed, and he can make things bad for ye.'

Matt rose, gazing at Jacko worriedly and the other boy winked.

'Tell him to send along a bottle of liquor,' Bridger joked as Matt turned to follow the sailor. 'He should treat his passengers better'n he does.'

Unshaven and weary-looking sailors were working on the deck repairing storm damage and wiping down the half-dozen small cannon the *Avon Pride* carried as Matt shuffled awkwardly after his guide. They glanced at the boy curiously, but without sympathy. The ship's mate, a small, vicious-faced man who stood beside the seaman at the large steering-wheel on the quarterdeck, stood aside to let him pass, glancing briefly at the boy's shackles. Matt lifted his feet over a high coaming step and then stood just inside the cabin that occupied the after end of the upper deck and was formed by the raised sterncastle. For a moment he could see nothing, his eyes blinded by light from a row of windows in the stern. Then he saw Captain Marlow, seated behind a long narrow table that extended down the centre of the compartment, and the boy drew himself upright, his shoulders back, trying to look defiant.

'You sent for me, Captain Marlow,' he said stiffly.

The man did not answer at once. His eyes were searching over the boy, noticing the soiled garments, the now grimy face, and when he spoke his tone was almost sad.

'I just wanted to see how ye were, lad,' he said with mocking sympathy. 'You been having a rough time forrard there and I was worrying about ye.'

The man's hypocrisy angered the boy and he burst out impulsively.

'You should worry about yourself,' he retorted, 'when you are being hanged for kidnapping me.'

The shipmaster's loose-muscled face spread into a wide, amused smile, and he shook his head as though chiding the boy.

'Now, that ain't being very friendly, lad,' he said regretfully, 'and it's foolish besides. You and me don't want to quarrel when we could be useful to each other.'

The man paused, to watch the boy speculatively, then he leant forward, his huge hands flat on the table.

'How'd ye like to be free of them irons, lad?' he asked softly. 'An' live aft here . . . wi' proper food and where ye can keep yerself clean? A lad like you—used to a proper home—'ll find it distasteful lying in that hole and wi' only them gallows-seed for company. How'd ye like that, boy?'

Matt stared at the man, distrusting him but thinking enviously of what he offered. To be free from the chafing shackles and the filth of the prison compartment would be wonderful, and the longing Matt could not suppress showed in his eyes. Captain Marlow saw the expression and smiled approvingly.

'I can see ye'd like that, Matt,' he said slyly. 'Ye're a sensible lad and I hates the thought of ye being broke in the plantations.' The man sat back, chuckling and looking at the boy with high delight. 'An' we'll give that rogue Parker and yer cousin a real shock, lad,' he went on. 'When I gets rid of my cargo and them scum forrard, we'll sail for Virginia and find yer uncle. I was tricked, lad . . . Same as you. Parker told me it was the other lad was called Matt Tuke and you was trying to do him harm. He wanted me to take ye out of the way and I was simple enough to let him fool me.'

'How do you know I am Matt Tuke now?' the boy demanded 'And why are you being so generous? I don't trust you, Captain Marlow.'

'And you've good cause not to,' the man agreed apologetically. 'It was coming down the river I got the truth, from that young scrag ye had with ye. He nigh tore my eyes out wi' his dirty claws, but he yells at me, saying he knows what my game is and that I'll hang for kidnapping ye. I been thinking all the passage, lad, and I can see how I've been tricked.' Captain Marlow paused, shaking his head at his own foolishness. 'I should ha' known, lad,' he ended. 'A fine lad like you!'

Matt had listened with growing disgust for the shipmaster's lying and now he looked his contempt.

'You knew who I was, Captain Marlow,' he exclaimed angrily. 'When I met you, you said you were a friend of my uncle and recognized me. Why do you tell such lies? What game are you playing? Do you think there is more profit in taking me to Virginia than to Barbados?'

The boy was furiously angry now and his voice rang with the scorn he felt, his eyes contemptuous. Captain Marlow scowled as he listened, his good nature gone and a sneer coming to his lips and eyes. He made a spitting sound, his fingers closing into his palms.

'Ye're a fool,' he said suddenly and viciously, 'like Parker said ye were.' He stopped, to glare at the boy, then went on contemptuously: 'All right, my lad. We'll stop fooling wi' each other. It's profit I'm after. . . . That's what I sail a ship for, and I go where I make the most. Ye're worth more if I carry ye to yer uncle than ye'd fetch in Barbados, and I want to trade to Virginia and the colonies. I'll make ye an offer that'll save ye from the plantations, and ye're mad if ye refuse it.'

'That at least is honest roguery,' Matt retorted. 'What's your offer, Captain Marlow?'

'Ye'll tell yer uncle I was tricked by Parker,' the man answered at once. 'And ye'll say I went out of my way to get ye to him. I've to be paid for that, and he's to reward me wi' helping me to get a cargo. That's what I want, and if ye agree to that I'll have them strike away yer irons and house ye aft.'

'And betray your fellow rogues,' Matt said, unable to hide his disgust. 'How do you know I would keep such a bargain? I could say I would and then tell the truth when I am free.'

The man snorted.

'Ye're not that sort,' he said with a sneer. 'Ye're the honest sort who keeps yer word. Else ye hadn't said that. I'll risk yer betraying me. . . . Is it a bargain, boy?'

Matt did not answer at once. He was being sorely tempted, for he thought of returning to his prison and being chained like an animal with horror. Then he remembered the plot to capture the *Avon Pride* and he could have cried with disappointment. If he agreed to Captain Marlow's bargain he had to break any promise he made to the shipmaster, for he could not betray Bridger and Jacko. The boy's mind worked feverishly, seeking a way through his problems, his whole body aching with the need for freedom and be rid of its dirt and discomfort. Yet if he promised he would be ashamed for ever, might even be the cause of this man's death and that of others aboard the ship.

'Well?' Captain Marlow demanded impatiently. 'Are ye grown so fond of filth and the company of these foul rogues that ye can't see what's best for yerself? I'd ha' thought ye'd jump at such an offer.'

Matt stared at the man, his mind still seeking a solution to his problem, and suddenly he saw what he must do. His loyalty was to Jacko, not to Sam Bridger or the three other prisoners. Bassett, Hardcastle, and even the Negro were criminals who deserved their punishment, and Sam Bridger—the only one of the four whom Matt liked—had said he could escape from Barbados easily. The ship need not be captured, and if Jacko were brought aft the plot to take her would be impossible. Everything relied on that strange boy, for only he could get free of his shackles and find the files. Matt could have laughed with relief.

'I will agree to your offer, Captain Marlow,' he cried suddenly and eagerly. 'But on one condition . . . You must include Jacko. He has to be freed also and come aft with me.'

Matt was smiling now, watching the man expectantly, and he saw the slack cheeks harden into an expression of such hatred that the boy stepped back in alarm, his fingers gripping at the chain between his wrists. Captain Marlow's face seemed to swell like a balloon and grow flushed, and his eyes glared at Matt in fury.

'I'd see ye in the blackest pit afore I'd do that,' he snarled, his fists thumping on the table. 'D'ye know what that young gaolbird did to me? Me, Captain Marlow, who's never let a man touch him without paying back! Nigh tore my eyes out of my head. Called me every foul name he learned in the gutter where he was bred! Ye must be mad to think I'd have that scum anywhere near me.'

'Then I'll have none of your offer,' Matt cried obstinately. 'And ye'll hang for what ye've done.'

The man rose then, towering over the table and towards the boy, hatred and spite in his eyes, contempt in his voice.

'Damn ye for the fool ye are,' he roared. 'I'll argue wi' ye no more, for ye're a bigger numskull than I thought. Ye can rot in Barbados, wi' the other scruff. I'll get what I want out of Parker and yer precious cousin.' He looked towards the cabin doorway, roaring for someone and the vicious-faced mate appeared.

'Take this fool out of my sight,' Captain Marlow shouted. 'I'll

B.J.—F

give him another fortnight of that place forrard, and ye'll see they get only what'll keep them alive. Clamp the hatch on them from now on. We've been too soft wi' them so far.'

Matt did not wait to be taken out of the cabin. He turned and shuffled as fast as his chains would allow to the doorway and on to the deck, then went forward, his face pale but his eyes defiant. He wanted to shout and say he was glad he was returning to his prison. He need not betray his fellow prisoners now. He saw Jacko watching him curiously, then Sam Bridger chuckled.

'You look like you and Marlow didn't hit it off, younker,' the man greeted. 'What did he want, Matt? Half yer uncle's fortune?'

Matt glowered his contempt for the shipmaster.

'He offered to carry me to Virginia, if I would agree to get my uncle to reward him and give him a cargo, and not betray his part in Parker's plot. If I agreed to this, I was to be given my freedom and live aft with the officers.'

Bridger smiled widely, nodding to say he had guessed this was Marlow's scheme, while Jacko giggled.

'Well, didn't ye say ye would?' Bridger asked. 'Ye could have lived comfortable for the rest of this voyage, and been helpful to us wi' being aft.'

Matt flushed, but he had to be honest.

'I would have accepted if he had let me bring Jacko aft, too,' he said defiantly. 'Ye know I have no liking for your plot, Sam.'

The man did not seem surprised or annoyed. He chuckled and nodded.

'An' he wouldn't have Jacko?' he said amusedly. 'So ye got all noble and turned his offer down . . . that it, lad?'

Matt nodded, hurt by the amusement in Bridger's voice and expression. Jacko gasped, gazing at the other boy in amazement. 'Ye what, chum?' he demanded. 'Ye turned down a chance to lie soft and eat proper food?'

'There's a babe in arms for ye, sprat,' Bridger said pityingly. 'He wouldn't have it if you wasn't there, mate.'

Jacko was gazing at Matt as though he were a complete stranger, thin fingers scratching at tangled black hair.

'Why, ye great simple,' he whispered throatily. 'Ye're crazy mad.'

But there was bewilderment in Jacko's voice as well as scorn. In all his precarious and harsh life nothing like this had ever occurred before and now he was at a loss for almost the first time in his cocksure existence. He saw the hurt expression in Matt's face and did not know what to do. Then he laughed, defending himself in this strange position.

'Why, mate,' he cried, 'ye don't think I'd ha' gone aft even if that swab had said I could? That'd have spoiled all the fun we're going to have. . . . What's the matter, chum? You looks sick.'

But Matt did not answer. He turned away and shuffled to the hatchway, hating Jacko for his laughter. A voice roared along the deck from aft.

'Get that scum below,' Captain Marlow bellowed, 'and see the hatch is closed. It's time they got a taste of what's coming to them.'

Jacko raised his small hand, fingers spread and the thumb at his nose. At least *he* knew how to retort to Captain Marlow.

MATT AMONG THIEVES

Captain Marlow's spiteful order to close the hatch on the prisoners did them a service: Jacko could resume his task of baring the two remaining nails at the foot of the bulkhead plank, without being seen from the deck. Enough light came into the compartment from between the planks of the hatch cover for the boy to see where he was digging and that afternoon he had completed the task. The wood round the three thick iron nails had been gouged away and the thick bulkhead plank could be drawn inward, away from its neighbours, to make a nine-inch-wide opening. Jacko would have levered the plank inward at once but Bridger stopped him.

'There's no hurry, cully,' he said. 'We've got another fortnight afore we want to take the ship over, and we'll take no foolish chances. We'll have a look at what's behind the bulkhead when it gets dark.'

Waiting for darkness was a strain on Jacko's and Matt's patience, but Sam Bridger was disclosing himself as a stern leader and a careful plotter. He used the hours of waiting to lecture Jacko on his next part in the venture.

'It's files we need most,' he said, 'and they won't be easy to get.'

'Where will they be?' Jacko demanded. 'I'll get 'em if I know where to go.'

'Don't be too cocky, younker,' Bridger chided. 'A ship ain't like being ashore. The carpenter'll have 'em in his tool-chest, and he likely keeps this in his berth. He'll berth aft, wi' the mate and steward and maybe the bosun, and getting down there ain't so simple. Ships is like graveyards, wi' every sound being heard. Sailors' ears pick up everything that don't belong to a ship going along, and they come looking when they hear strange noises. You got to move like a savage after a scalp, and don't ever move until ye're sure it's safe.'

'Ye've never seen me working,' Jacko boasted. 'I could take the bed from under ye and ye wouldn't know it was took.'

'I seen enough of ye to know ye've been trained in all kinds of thievery,' Bridger agreed. 'But you ain't in a town, where people ain't on lookout like they are aboard a vessel, so don't you talk foolish. . . . Ye've got to know where ye're going and where to search when ye gets there.'

The man began to describe the ship to Jacko, and the boy listened intently. Matt was impressed by Bridger's description, for the man had noticed a dozen things the boy had walked past and not seen. He had noticed that a hatch cover had been lifted off, to let the warmer air of the now fine weather into the hold, drying out any dampness caused by the storm; this opening would be Jacko's way out of the hold and on to the upper deck.

'That's if they leave it off during the night,' Bridger explained. 'It's close by where whoever's in charge of the deck will pass, and the man at the wheel, so you've got to pick your time for getting out. Eight bells at midnight's yer best time, when the watch is changing and men are moving around in the dark. Getting back into the hold ain't going to be easy neither, but not so dangerous as getting on deck.'

Bridger described the quarterdeck to the boy, telling him to have a good look aft the next day when they were on deck for their solitary meal, and to notice where the main hatch was open and how he would get to a canopied companion-way that led down into the officers' quarters. There was no moon for another three weeks, the man explained, and with the ship carrying all her sails the deck would be dark. So, if he was as good as he claimed to be and took no unnecessary risks, Jacko should be able to get to the companion-way and reach the cabins there undiscovered.

'You don't miss much, do you, Sam!' Matt exclaimed admiringly. 'I never thought about the moon.'

Bridger chuckled.

'You aren't a desperate character like me and Jacko,' he retorted good humouredly. 'An' I'll lay a bet ye never even noticed where Marlow keeps the muskets and pistols when ye was in his cabin.'

Matt blushed for his neglect. He tried to see the cabin again, but all he could remember were the row of stern windows, Captain Marlow's face glowering at him and the shipmaster's great hands on the oaken table. Then he remembered seeing several wooden chests lashed to ring-bolts in the deck, and what might have been weapons stacked in a corner of the cabin. Bridger shrugged his shoulders when the boy described these things.

'You won't never make a thief, lad,' he said regretfully. 'If it was Jacko who'd been there we'd know what Marlow had for his breakfast, never mind where the arms is kept. But I expect he keeps them in his berth. He's the sort wouldn't trust a pistol out of his sight, for his crew ain't in love wi' him as far as I can see!' The man paused, then went on, 'But that's for later on. It's files we wants now and they won't be in Marlow's cabin. We'll find weapons when the time comes.'

'It's dark now, Sam,' Jacko said eagerly. 'What about seeing what's behind the bulkhead?'

They all listened, hearing no sound outside the compartment, except the lazy creaking of block sheaves and ropes and the low mutter of water along the ship's side.

'Go ahead, younker,' Bridger agreed. 'But easy as she goes, an' don't snap off yer dagger getting it out.'

'I'll lever it out,' Jacko whispered. 'You be ready to grip the edge of the plank as it comes, Matt.'

The two boys knelt facing the bulkhead, and Jacko put the point of his dagger between the plank to be taken out and its neighbour, levering carefully. He whispered a warning and Matt groped, then gripped with his finger tips. He held the edge of the plank, until Jacko worked his dagger point again and the plank came inward, Matt gripping behind it and drawing it towards himself slowly.

'Don't pull too hard, or too far, lad,' Bridger warned. 'We don't want the nails to come away at the top.'

Jacko was already groping behind the plank and now he called out excitedly.

'It feels like sacking, Sam,' he whispered. 'Bales of something, and smells like cloth.'

'Yer nose is right,' the man said with satisfaction, 'It'll be cloth. They'd stow that in the 'tween decks where it wouldn't get damp. Slit the bale, younker, and make sure.'

Jacko drew the dagger blade down on the hessian, then felt again, crying out jubilantly.

'It's cloth, mate. I can feel the rolls. I'll pull some out.

'You leave it be,' Bridger ordered. 'We've done enough for now. Just feel higher up and make sure it's bales on top as well, then put that plank back. You ain't moving around this ship until ye know where to go and how to get there.'

Jacko protested, but Matt was again impressed by Bridger's caution. The two boys pressed the plank back and Bridger gave Matt a handful of softened ship's biscuits he had prepared.

'Fill in the holes where Jacko dug out the timber,' the man instructed, 'then nobody'll notice what we've been doing.' He waited until Matt had completed this task, then told the boys to go to sleep. 'Specially you, sprat,' he said. 'You got a long night tomorrow.'

When they were brought on deck for their meal the next day Matt was even more impressed by Bridger's planning. With their guard out of hearing distance, the man whispered to Jacko, telling him what he must remember of the ship's deck.

'Ye can see where the hatch is lifted off,' he said, 'an' it looks like it wasn't closed down last night . . . it's just like I saw it yesterday. You notice how the mate walks to and fro across the quarterdeck, aft of the hatch. And the wheel is only eight or ten feet away from where ye have to get out. The mate'll stay more on the weather side, and the hatch is off on the leeward side, so that helps ye. And the companion-way is on that side. You slides over the coaming and lies flat against it, until the mate's on the far side, and then nip down.'

'I don't see how he can do it,' Matt said apprehensively. 'He'll be discovered.'

Jacko grinned.

'I done worse jobs,' he said confidently, 'getting into houses and opening doors for my mates, and ye'd be surprised how blind some are.'

That night Jacko proved his skill as a thief. When the ship's bell struck two double raps to announce ten o'clock, Bridger gave the order to open the bulkhead and for Jacko to clear a way into the hold. The plank was eased inward, Matt holding the bottom end up while Jacko ripped open a bale near the deckhead. He drew out rolls of fine cloth, placing these inside the compartment, until the bale was half emptied and the boy could climb up to the top of the stacked cargo. Bridger passed the rolls of cloth up and Jacko thrust them out of sight under the deck beams, whispering that there was a clear eighteen inches of space between the top of the cargo and the beams.

'Now mind, younker,' Bridger warned softly. 'Wait till the watch is changing at midnight. Get aft there now, and make sure the hatch cover's still off, then wait. If they catches ye while ye're on deck, say ye came up through this hatch here. Don't let them know we got a plank out.'

'I ain't a greenhorn,' Jacko retorted, sounding excited. 'I'll be on my way now mates.'

Bridger told Matt to drop the end of the plank, but to leave it so he could get a grip again, and the boy obeyed. Bridger chuckled in the darkness.

'Reg'ler young dodger,' he said admiringly, 'born for the job! He'll get them files.'

'He has just been born into roguery,' Matt protested, 'and he could learn more honest ways if he had the opportunity.'

Bridger chuckled again, his eyes seeking the darkness for the boy's face.

'He wouldn't never be satisfied doing honest work, younker,' he said, 'an' ye'd never learn him. I seen others like him, brought up from they was babes to prig on them who's got something. To Jacko thieving is natural now, and them what works for a living are fools. He couldn't stop hisself stealing if you was to offer him yer uncles' plantation . . for he'd only go after bigger game. He's out of the city jungle, lad, and thieving and being smarter than other folks is meat and drink to him. I'll swear he'd rob you if he saw something he wanted, and I'd say he's as near loving you as he has ever been wi' anybody.'

'You are wrong, Sam,' the boy argued hotly. 'I am sure you are. I would trust Jacko with anything I possessed.'

'An' ye'd lose it, lad,' the man answered pityingly. 'You done him a good turn there in Taunton, and he'll pay ye back by getting ye to Virginia . . . but don't you leave anything valuable around or he'll have it. And getting you to yer uncle is getting his own back on this rogue Parker. Like taking this ship is getting back at Marlow. Ye'll never understand or cure them that's been brought up like he's been, like ye'd never make a sheep-dog out of a wolf, lad.'

Matt did not answer, but he held stubbornly to what he believed about the other boy. Jacko had just never had the opportunities to be honest, but when they did reach Virginia he would have. Colonel Tuke would employ him and he would become an honest citizen, become Matt's loyal follower. But even as Matt told himself this would happen, he remembered how Jacko had received the information that Matt had sacrificed the chance to be taken to his uncle by Captain Marlow. Both Jacko and Bridger had thought him a fool, a simple-minded child, for not playing a trick on the shipmaster, taking what he offered, then helping them to steal the *Avon Pride*. They had not understood that one must be honest, even with enemies.

Four sharp double raps of the ship's bell announcing midnight and the end of a watch interrupted the boy's thoughts, and he sat up listening for sounds that would tell him that Jacko had been discovered as he tried to crawl out of the hold. Matt could hear the men breathing in the darkness, feel their tenseness as the moments passed. Footsteps thumped overhead as the watch changed and men being relieved went forward to find corners where they would sleep, voices sounded distantly. Someone uttered an oath of annoyance, then the sounds of movement ceased and there was only the muttering of the water and the creak of block sheaves.

'He's out!' Bridger whispered.

The next two hours were agony to Matt Tuke. He was listening every moment, trembling with anxiety for the absent boy, imagining him creeping into the companion, down the steep ladder to where the ship's carpenter would sleep, groping in darkness to try and find where the tool-chest was. It seemed an impossible task and Matt did not believe anyone could succeed. A hiss from Bridger, then the boy heard a tapping against the bulkhead and he felt for the edge of the plank. He drew it out, to hear movement inside the hold. A small dark figure slid down, backing into the compartment.

'Ye get the files, sprat?' Bridger whispered, and Jacko laughed.

'It was easy, mate,' he answered throatily. 'Sailors must be blind and deaf. . . . I could ha' taken the ship without them knowing.'

'The files, lad,' Bridger demanded urgently, his shackles clinking as he reached his hands towards the boy.

'Here ye are, Sam,' Jacko answered. 'I took two.'

'Get that plank back,' the man ordered, 'and slip into yer irons again, younker. Ye done a proper job tonight.'

'What happened, Jacko?' Matt demanded. 'It has been awful waiting here.'

He could almost see the other boy's grin and the delighted expression in his eyes.

'It was fun,' Jacko answered, his voice charged with pride. 'I got out of the hold when Sam says I should and nobody knew I was there. I has to hide behind the canopy while someone comes up and another man goes below, then I creeps down and hears somebody snoring. There's a place wi' a table an' benches, wi' a man sleeping on a bench. I feels round the walls, finding doors and some cupboards, but there ain't no chests.'

'Ye'd be in the mess room,' Bridger told him. 'Go on, cully.'

'I got into one cabin,' Jacko continued, 'and it's empty. Nobody there. I finds a chest and feels in it, but there's only clothes and a pistol and a bag of money.'

'Ye left them there,' Bridger said threateningly.

The boy laughed softly.

'I did, Sam,' he said. 'Then I tried the next cabin and I'm lucky. I finds two chests and one's got tools in it.'

'Was the carpenter there?' Matt asked, awed by Jacko's daring.

'Snoring like a fat sow,' the other boy answered. 'Wouldn't have woke up if I'd pulled his nose. I had to take out a lot of tools before I felt the files, then put the tools back.'

Matt uttered a sigh, relieved and admiring. He felt something being pushed into one of his hands and gripped a sticky lump.

'What's this, Jacko?' he whispered.

'Raisins, chum,' the other answered. 'I found a chest full of them in the mess room.'

'Ye young fool,' Bridger whispered angrily. 'I told ye to touch nothing but the files.'

'There was a chest full,' the boy said. 'Wasn't no harm in taking some.'

'There's harm in not doing what ye're told,' the man retorted angrily. 'Ye could spoil our chances, taking things that might be noticed. Ye'd best learn to carry out yer orders or you an' me'll part company.'

To Matt's surprise, Jacko muttered that he was sorry, sounding subdued. Bridger grunted.

'We'll let it go this time,' he said sourly, 'and hope ye haven't ruined things. Ye did well, getting the files, but don't ever do anything but what ye'er told again.' The man paused, then said, 'Anyhow, there'll be no need for ye to go on deck again, not until we're ready to take the ship.'

'What about weapons, Sam?' Jacko asked meekly.

'Ye can crawl round the hold later on,' the man answered. 'There should be something there that'll serve. All we need are a few cudgels and if we plans this proper and move fast when we start there needn't be any shooting.'

The conversation ended then, Jacko curling up on the deck and going to sleep, while Matt lay on his back, thinking of Jacko's feat and how he had accepted Sam Bridger's chiding. The boy was impressed by the scar-faced sailor, admiring him, and this troubled Matt. He wanted to take Jacko away from such people, away from a life of dishonesty. If Bridger became a hero in Jacko's eyes, the man would lead him into piracy and to a hangman's rope.

Bridger and the counterfeiter, Hardcastle, began work on their shackles the next night, in darkness. They were not to file right through the bolts securing their wrist and ankle irons, but leave enough of the metal to hold the irons, the file cuts being filled in with softened ship's biscuit worked to a paste to conceal the handiwork. It took the two men a week to complete their task, then the files were passed to Matt and the Negro. Bassett's shackles were to be left as they were, for Bridger distrusted the poisoner and said he would only be a burden when the time came to take the ship. Bassett was being kept in a state of abject fear by the sailor, threatened with sudden death if he ever again tried to attract Captain Marlow's attention, and called every sort of foul traitor, although he denied having any such intention.

'We know what ye'd do, ye rat,' Bridger told him. 'Ye'd think to get yer freedom by betraying us to Marlow, but ye don't know his sort. He'd sell ye just the same, and he'd do no more than flog us for plotting against him. We're worth money to that dirty spiriter and he'll not spoil his goods. Then, we'd get ye in Barbados, Bassett.'

The other man wept in his denials, but he was cowed. His plumpness had gone, his face becoming pale and slack, and he spent most of the time lying with his back to the others. When he was spoken to at all, it was contemptuously and harshly, for, Matt discovered, even rogues like Hardcastle detested poisoners and amateur criminals like Bassett.

Matt learned a great deal about criminals as the *Avon Pride* sailed across the Atlantic; for Bridger, Hardcastle, and Jacko entertained each other and passed the hours recounting their exploits. Bridger had been a smuggler in the English Channel and had served aboard pirate ships, and even Matt was stirred by the tales he told. Hardcastle, to Bridger's urging, described the tricks of counterfeiters, explaining all the time in his lugubrious voice that he had been forced into crime because society would not repay a poet for his labours. But Jacko's tales, told in his throaty, boasting voice, shocked Matt, for the thin-faced boy had been a thief and pickpocket since he was a young child. He could not remember having parents, and had only memories of sleeping where he could find a corner, eating when he could steal, and being trained in crime by men who used boys to enter houses by the windows and open doors for the robbers. Jacko had learned to crawl through the smallest openings and move around a house like a ghost, as he had learned to pick pockets and remove valuables under the owner's very eyes. His adventure into the countryside as a highwayman's spy had been his first experience outside towns, his first experience, too, of being caught and punished, though Matt had saved him from the worst of this punishment.

What horrified Matt as he listened was Jacko's pride in his skill as a thief, his delight in having tricked unsuspecting people, his scorn for those who lived honest lives.

Jacko's heroes, Matt realized, were thieves and tricksters who preyed on honest people, and now the boy had found a new hero in Sam Bridger. His ambition was to sail with Bridger, to be a rollicking pirate, for the man made piracy sound like a continuous adventure, where riches poured from plundered ships and freebooters were the boldest and merriest sailors afloat. Matt pitied Jacko for being so easily gulled and he argued with Bridger to try and show the other boy that roguery was not all excitement and jollification.

'It doesn't always mean getting rich and having adventures,' Matt protested after Bridger had described another exciting capture. 'And it hasn't done much for you, Sam. Pirates are taken and hanged every week, and none of them keeps their plunder. Have you ever heard of one who took his share and lived comfortably afterwards?'

The man laughed and Jacko looked at Matt pityingly.

'Who wants to live comfortable, younker,' Bridger demanded, 'while there's jolly shipmates to drink wi', fat prizes to take, and the Queen's Navy to make fools of? There have been pirates who carried their plunder home and set up as fine gentlemen, and maybe one day ye'll see me acting the squire back in Somerset. But that'll be when I'm too old and stiff to swing a cutlass or storm aboard a ship. A long way ahead, lad, and if I swings from a rope afore I get old, why, I'll have had a merry life while it lasted, and a true gentleman of fortune takes what comes and don't grouse.'

Matt was shocked by such words and worried for Jacko's sake. But he could not help admiring Bridger as well. The man was a true leader and his plans to capture the *Avon Pride* were being made as carefully as any general approaching an enemy would plan a battle. He had the whole attack plotted in detail, even scratching a plan of the ship on the dirty deck planks of their prison, to show each of them where they had to go when the attempt was made. Their success depended on everyone doing exactly what Bridger ordered, and on the hatch cover being left off so that they could get out of the hold quickly. Bridger himself would go first, to subdue the mate, or whoever was in charge of the ship that night. Jacko would be second, making for the seaman at the wheel and threatening him with his dagger to prevent an alarm being raised. Hardcastle and the Negro were to reach the great cabin and overcome Captain Marlow while he was asleep. Matt had the least dangerous part, and even as he was relieved to know he was not to attack anyone he was annoyed at being given such an easy task. He was to close the doors into the companion-way that led to the officers' quarters under the quarterdeck, and then stand by these doors, unless any of the crew appeared and resisted the capture of their ship.

'Ye ain't the sort for cutting throats, younker,' Bridger told the boy good-naturedly, 'too soft-hearted by far. Yer task is as important as any. There'll be three of them down there, and they're the only ones who'll stand by Marlow. If we batten them down below, we'll have no trouble with the crew. They hates Marlow and when they know we've got him, wi' the mate and that red-headed bosun, they're more likely to raise a cheer. It's them who's aft we got to handle.'

Matt, with the others, had seen how much the *Avon Pride's*

crew detested their officers, and with good cause. Even at a time when the crews of merchant ships as well as men-of-war were treated worse than animals, conditions for the men aboard the *Avon Pride* were brutally cruel. They were fed like beasts and driven like slaves by the small fierce-eyed mate and the bosun, a huge giant of a man with a shock of red hair and a face bruised and scarred worse than Sam Bridger's. Marlow's language to the men was seldom anything but the foullest abuse, and the slightest delay in carrying out an order, or any lack of obedience, brought quick punishment from a wooden belaying-pin the mate always carried, or from the bosun's great fists. Worse punishments were frequent and a man who did not move fast enough to satisfy Marlow during the storm was sent out along the bowsprit, to cling there till the ship drove into heavy seas and the unfortunate sailor was washed away. Three men had been flogged since the *Avon Pride* had sailed from England, and the prisoners had been brought on deck to stand with the seamen and watch this punishment being inflicted. Matt had almost vomited as he saw the bosun bring the lash down on the victim's naked back, the seaman slung by his wrists from the rigging so that his toes just touched the deck. After thirty lashes the man's back was a mass of raw, bleeding flesh and he was long since unconscious. Marlow, standing on the stern-castle with the mate, both behind small guns loaded with buckshot that were used for repelling boarders and now prevented the crew from interfering, had roared for the victim to be cut down and dragged forward. The boy had heard the muttering around him, heard Bridger taunting the seamen for allowing a shipmate to be tortured like this, and felt sick.

Sam Bridger was working on that hatred as the *Avon Pride* sailed westward. As the prisoners squatted round the tub of food every day, he was taunting the guards and any seaman working near by, telling them they were a poor lot of swabs who let themselves be treated as they were, that the ship's cargo could make them all rich, and that if they were any sort of men they would mutiny. Bridger's daring to say what he did frightened Matt, for omeone might tell Marlow what the man said. The sailors who heard him scowled, but Bridger was sure his words were having an effect.

'I hope he flogs a few more afore we gets to the islands,' he said callously. 'They'll be all the more willing to help us when we takes the ship. They're a poor crowd of swabs, but they'll serve to sail her to New Providence and we'll find a proper crew there.'

The man had decided when to make their attempt: when the *Avon Pride* was close to the West Indies, and the ocean crossed.

'Marlow's making for Hispaniola,' Bridger told the other prisoners, 'to go inside the Leeward Islands and make for Barbados. We waits until we raises Hispaniola, and then we're handy for the Bahamas and New Providence.'

The man was content to wait, though the days brought increasing fears to Matt and affected Jacko even more. To lie in their prison, shackled and inactive, irritated the boy, and he was demanding every night that he should go into the hold and find weapons, make sure the hatch was still open, or finding other reasons for action. Bridger just grinned and told the boy to take life easy.

'Soon's I see signs that Marlow's expecting to raise the island is time enough,' he chided. 'We don't want to do anything that'll spoil our chances.'

Jacko sulked, but he did as he was told. Matt continued to worry, afraid that some keen-eyed seaman would notice where their shackles had been filed, or that Marlow would send for him to renew his offer. The shipmaster might even agree to having Jacko aft, and if this offer were refused he would become suspicious. Jacko, Matt knew, would not forgo this adventure now, for taking the ship and paying Captain Marlow back for kidnapping him meant more to the dark-haired boy than the freedom they would win.

'What are ye going to do wi' that fat swab when we take the ship?' Jacko demanded one night as they lay talking of their plans. 'We should string him up, Sam.'

Bridger laughed, amused by the boy's vindictive tone.

'We'll give him to Matt,' he answered jokingly; 'it's him that'
been treated worse. What do ye say, younker?'

'I don't want him killed!' Matt exclaimed. 'Couldn't we pu
him in a boat and send him away?'

Jacko snorted, but Bridger grinned.

'And have him get to one of the islands where he'd find a man
o'-war to come after us?' he said. 'I told ye yer too soft, younker.
He watched the boy amusedly, then said, 'If Hardcastle don't hav
to finish him off to keep him quiet, we'll find somewhere to pu
him. It ain't only him . . . there'll be the mate and the bosun, ar
maybe some others who don't want to sail wi' us. We'll land 'er
on one of the small islands where they ain't likely to be foun
for a bit. I ain't one for slaughter when it's not needed, and it'
punish Marlow more to see us sailing his ship away than if w
strung him up.'

Matt uttered a sigh of relief. He hated the shipmaster but he di
not wish to see the man murdered. Jacko's ferocity horrified th
boy, but he told himself that was only the other boy trying
show off. Jacko liked to shock him and would not kill so col
bloodedly.

'I seen them who slaughtered just for the sake of killing,' Bri
ger was saying now, 'but it ain't a wise thing to do. It gets th
Navy after ye. Like they went after Blackbeard. I likes a battle
well as the next, but I ain't bloodthirsty like some. I'd as so
watch Marlow's face when we puts him over the side.'

'And the sooner we do that the better,' Jacko growled throa
ily. 'I'll be screaming mad if I don't get out of here soon.'

He was allowed to get out when Bridger reckoned the *Av
Pride* was within two days' sailing from the island of Hispanio
The man watched for signs that Marlow expected to sight t
islands, and when the prisoners came on deck one day to se
look-out was being kept from the foremast, he knew it was ti
to move. That night Jacko slipped out of his shackles and crawl
into the hold to search for weapons. He returned to say he co

find only three short iron bars, which he had left on top of the cargo, to be picked up when they left their prison.

'They'll serve,' Bridger approved. 'One for me, and Hardcastle and the nigger can have the other. Matt don't need anything and Jacko has his dagger.'

Thirty-six hours later, with daylight fully come, a voice sang out loudly from aloft, and Bridger sat up, raising a hand for silence.

'Where away?' Captain Marlow roared from aft and the lookout sang back, his words clear to the now tense prisoners.

'Fine on the starboard bow, sir!' the call came, and Bridger laughed contentedly.

'Mind me to thank Marlow for making a good landfall,' he said mockingly. 'We'll take her tonight, mates.'

7

THE TAKING OF THE 'AVON PRIDE'

They left the prison compartment at one o'clock the nex
morning, an hour, Sam Bridger hoped, when the watch on dec
would have found corners where they could steal some extr
sleep in the fine weather, and there would be only whoever wa
in charge of the watch, the helmsman, and a look-out on th
forecastle alert. Before they left their prison, Bridger warned th
miserable Bassett that if he tried to raise an alarm and war

anyone of the attack on the ship someone would return and 'tear his ears off and stuff them down his traitorous throat', a threat that reduced the frightened man to grovelling assurances that he would not stir from where he lay or utter a sound. Bridger also addressed his small band, telling them that if the crew should be alarmed and come to the help of their officers they were to submit at once.

'Ain't no sense in dying,' the sailor declared, 'and if they all come against us we're done. Marlow ain't going to do more than flog us . . . and not much of that either. We're valuable merchandise and wouldn't be worth so much wi' our backs torn wi' the lash. If we fails this time we'll get out of Barbados somehow.'

Matt was relieved by these orders. He did not know if he was afraid or not, for courage was something he had never considered; it had been called on only for sport until now. But he hated the thought of having to kill someone, of adding murder to this crime of stealing a ship. He was shocked by Jacko's ferocious threats of what he would do to Captain Marlow, made nervous by the cruel expression on the man Hardcastle's face when he had been told he was to stop the shipmaster from making any noise or reaching a weapon. Jacko's threats were too extravagant to be taken seriously, but the counterfeiter was sinister and frightening. The boy prayed that Bridger's plans to take the ship without fighting would be successful.

Bridger was at the head of the small party when they left their prison, with Jacko close behind him. Hardcastle followed Jacko, then the Negro, with Matt last. He crawled over the bales of cloth, keeping his head down to avoid the deck beams, following the others by the sound of their breathing and their bodies dragging over the bales. It was pitch dark in the hold, the odours of cargo and bilge water stinging the eyes. Sounds were nerve-rackingly mysterious, as though the ship herself was whispering a warning of danger, the water muttering against her sides like a gossiping audience. Now and then a sudden rustling and scampering startled the boy, rats squeaking as they were disturbed

in their nests among the cargo. Matt's forehead was wet with perspiration and his fingers clutched tightly as he drew himself
forward.

He flattened as someone whispered in front of him, but it was
Bridger, warning his followers that they had reached the end of
the bales and were coming on to wooden packing-cases, and must
move more carefully. They went on again, Matt feeling the
harder surface. His stockinged foot struck a corner and he almost
cried out with the pain. They had all removed their shoes before
leaving their prison, after they had filed through the last of the
iron bolts holding their arms and leg shackles closed. Now,
wincing at the pain of the blow, Matt went on. Another whispered
warning came from ahead and the boy stopped, feeling a cool
breeze against his head. He looked up to see a lighter patch against
the darkness in the hold, and he knew the hatch cover was still
off, the way to the upper deck open. There would be no turning
back now, for the success of their plot had relied on the hatch
being still open. If it had been closed they could not have hoped
to reach the upper deck unobserved.

Then, as Matt stared up at the opening, seeing a star gleaming
above him, footsteps sounded, a slow pacing step that seemed to
press through the deck planks on to his head. Whoever was in
charge of the ship was walking across the quarterdeck, placing
his feet slowly so as not to disturb those who slept in the cabins
aft of the hold. The footsteps passed to the ship's side, to pause
there, then returned across the quarterdeck. Matt heard Bridger
whispering and drew himself forward, lying beside the Negro.

'It's that swab of a bosun,' Bridger was saying. 'I have to get
him quick, for he's a lusty rogue.' He paused, listening to the
footsteps now on the side of the deck away from the opening,
then spoke again. 'Ye all know what to do,' he said. 'He'll walk
across again, and when he turns to go back next time I nip out and
lie against the hatch coaming. I wait till he comes back the next
time, then when his back's to me I jump on him. You be ready to
get out, Jacko. When you hear me hit him, get out and make for

the man at the wheel. Let him feel yer dagger. You others know what to do and do it quick. Don't let Marlow shout or we're done.'

'He's coming back,' Jacko whispered warningly.

The bosun—if Bridger's guess was right and it was that huge red-headed bully Matt had seen ill-using the crew so brutally—was pacing back and forth across the clear expanse of deck between the hatchway into the hold and the raised sterncastle, pausing each time he reached the ship's side, to gaze outward at the night-hidden sea, or upward at the canvas pyramiding against the star-scattered sky. He was now crossing the deck, towards the side where the hatch was open and the small group of men and boys crouched on top of the cargo, passing some eight feet from where they lay. Matt felt rather than saw the man's shadow, then the footsteps were going towards the ship's side. They paused, then returned, and as they receded to the other side of the deck Bridger rose. He peered across the ship, seeing a figure against the night, a dim glow that he knew was the candlelight inside the compass box. The bosun's back was to him, and Bridger rose higher, to step over the raised coaming and then drop and lie flat against it, a short iron bar gripped in one powerful fist.

This had been the most dangerous moment for the attackers, and those in the hold held their breaths as Bridger made his move. Jacko uttered a low sigh of relief and Matt put a hand to his forehead, wiping away some of the sweat. They were all listening intently, waiting for the bosun to return across the quarterdeck. As he passed the open hatchway Jacko came to his hands and knees, waiting for Bridger to begin the attack. There was a slither of movement through the deck planks, a soft padding noise as Bridger came behind the unsuspecting victim. The man must have heard the movement, for he made to turn. He was too late. Bridger's arm rose and came down, the iron bar crushing on the bosun's head. Matt heard the gasp of pain, then Jacko seemed to be shot upwards through the opening. He leapt and was gone, the tall thin figure of Hardcastle rising, the thicker, broader Negro beside him. They scrambled over the coaming and Matt rose and threw himself on to the deck. He heard a familiar chuckle.

'Don't fall over this thing, younker,' Bridger whispered warningly. 'Stay beside the companion when ye've secured it, lad, and sing out if ye hear anyone moving below.'

The man passed across the deck, towards where Jacko stood behind a startled seaman, uttering ferocious threats of what would happen if the helmsman made a sound. But the man could only stare at Sam Bridger, his mouth gaping.

'You was in irons, mate,' the seaman gasped and Bridger laughed softly.

'We bit through them, mate,' he said humorously. 'Now you just keep steering and nobody'll harm ye.' He turned to Jacko. 'Take yer dagger away, sprat,' he said, 'and see what's happened to Marlow.'

Across the quarterdeck Matt Tuke was completing his part in the taking of the *Avon Pride*. It was a simple enough task, though Bridger had instructed the boy as carefully as though their whole success depended on him. Matt, his fingers made clumsy by excitement, had to close two small doors in the canopy over the companion-way that led downward to the cabin Jacko had raided so successfully. The boy had studied the doors when he had been on deck for his daily meal and now he lifted two small hooks that held them open, closed them and drew an iron hasp on one door over a small hoop on the other. He felt in a pocket, to find a short wooden peg that he thrust into the hoop, securing the hasp and preventing anyone from pushing the doors open from inside the canopy. The peg—another of Bridger's carefully planned details—had been cut from plank in the prison compartment.

His task completed, breathing quickly as his heart thumped with excitment, Matt turned to peer across the quarterdeck, waiting for sounds of struggle. He recognized Bridger's tall figure, standing near the man at the wheel, and nothing was happening. The *Avon Pride* was sailing along as though the attack had never taken place, with only the little muttering and creaking sounds a ship makes in fine weather. Her deck planks glowed a lighter hue against the night, her sails rose ghostlily, but not a man appeared forward of the quarterdeck. The boy felt suddenly disappointed. He had imagined all sorts of things—a desperate struggle, bloodshed and noise of battle—and instead, Sam Bridger was laughing, the familiar soft chuckling laugh Matt knew so well. He said something to the man at the wheel and was answered in a voice full of respect, as though the man wanted to show how eager he was to do what Bridger wanted. Then Bridger came towards Matt.

'How was that, younker?' he demanded, smiling widely. 'Like taking pennies from a blind man?'

'Where is everyone?' the boy asked, still bewildered by the easy victory. 'What have they done to Captain Marlow?'

The man chuckled.

'The watch is somewhere around,' he said. 'I sent Jacko in to find out what happened to Marlow.'

Jacko appeared, walking with a swagger and grinning when he came near.

'He won't make no trouble,' he announced.

'Is he dead?' Matt asked anxiously. 'They didn't kill him, Jacko?'

'Wouldn't have been no loss if they had,' the other boy answered. ' 'Cept that I want to tell him what I think of him. No, he's tied up in his bunk, wi' his mouth stuffed wi' bed-clothes and his eyes spitting. He'll be sorry he ever listened to that swab Parker.'

Bridger went to where the huddled figure of the bosun still lay near the hatchway, kneeling down and feeling over the body. He rose, holding a pistol he had taken from his victim.

'Wearing a wool cap that saved his skull,' he said. 'Feel along the rail for a length of rope, Jacko. We best tie him up before he gets his senses back.'

Jacko went towards the ship's side and Bridger stretched his arms wide and took a long deep breath.

'This smells better 'n that foul hole we were in, Matt,' he said contentedly, 'and we'll be in New Providence in a week, wi' the cargo sold and our pockets full of guineas.' He grinned at the boy. 'How d'ye like being a gentleman of fortune, younker? Ye don't have to go to Virginia to get rich.'

Matt looked alarmed.

'I don't want to be a pirate,' he exclaimed. 'I will be able to get to Virginia, Sam?'

The man laughed softly, placing a large hand on the boy's shoulder.

'Ye'll be there afore ye're much older, lad,' he promised. 'There's ships back and forward from New Providence all the time. Traders who don't mind buying plunder to sell in the colonies. I'd like to be there and see this rogue Parker's face when ye steps ashore, lad.'

Matt had not thought of this. He exclaimed apprehensively

'I hadn't thought about that, Sam. What will happen to Parker and my cousin?'

'Hanged for kidnapping ye, I suppose,' the man told him surprised by the question. 'And they deserves to hang. If we hadn't taken this ship, ye'd have slaved yer life out in Barbado while they was living like lords.'

'But I don't want Peter to be punished,' Matt cried. 'It would kill Aunt Janet if he were hanged. I must tell Uncle Franklyn not to have him arrested.'

Bridger scratched his head, puzzled for the moment, then he shrugged his shoulders.

'You was born to be made a fool of, lad,' he said at last. 'If I was in your shoes I'd have 'em all strung up . . . Marlow as well. He looked beyond the boy as Jacko appeared. 'Find that rope younker?'

Jacko had cut a length of rope from where he had found a co on a belaying-pin. Bridger secured the still unconscious bosu then dragged him aft against the sterncastle.

'See if ye can find a lantern in Marlow's berth,' he told Jacko 'and some weapons. It's time we roused out them swabs forrard. Bring Hardcastle back wi' ye.'

There was an authority in the man's voice that brought a startled expression to Jacko's eyes, but he laughed throatily.

'Aye, aye, sir,' he answered, making a mock salute.

'That's right, younker,' Bridger approved. 'It's Captain Bridger now and ye'll bend on a "sir" when ye answers me.'

He went towards the wheel, Jacko hurrying to the door into the sterncastle. Matt was left beside the canopy, with new worries. He was thinking of what Bridger had said, that Parker and Peter would be hanged for having him kidnapped. That would be awful, for Aunt Janet's heart would break with the shame. Rather than have this happen Matt would not go near Virginia, nor claim his inheritance. He must make his uncle let Peter go back to England, even if it meant that Parker escaped punishment. The boy's thoughts were interrupted by a light appearing inside Captain Marlow's cabin. Jacko came on deck, carrying a lantern in one hand and a naked cutlass in the other. The boy had armed himself with a vengeance, for two large pistols stuck out of the top of his breeches and another was slung on a cord round his neck. He strutted towards Bridger, delighted with himself. Hardcastle followed him, two pistols in his belt and carrying another pair. Bridger took one of the weapons from Hardcastle, then told the man to go forrard and rouse out the crew.

'Shoot anyone who don't do what he's told,' he ordered, 'and, Jacko, give Matt one of them pistols.'

'You'll have no bother with the crew, Captain,' the man at the wheel said earnestly. 'Not when they knows you've got Marlow tied up.'

Matt took the pistol Jacko offered, hoping that the helmsman was right and that no one would make trouble. But he watched carefully as Jacko and Hardcastle went forward, Jacko holding the lantern high and calling on the sleeping seamen to 'Lift yer lazy bodies and muster aft to meet yer new captain'. Figures were appearing under the sails, rising from the corners where they had been asleep, prodded to faster movement by the point of Jacko's cutlass. The boy was abusing the sleep-dazed and bewildered men with ripe oaths, answering their questions with bullying humour. Men began to come aft, asking each other what had happened, and calling out. Then they saw Sam Bridger standing in front of the wheel, feet apart and his shoulders squared aggressively, his pistols pointed.

'That'll do ye,' he sang out authoritatively. 'Keep where ye are till I tells ye to move.'

' 'It's them was being transported,' a man exclaimed in amazement. 'They've got the ship.'

'Aye, .mate,' Bridger answered. 'We done what you would have done weeks ago if ye'd been only half men.'

'Some of us would have took her,' a voice growled, 'only others was too chicken-hearted. . . . What ye done wi' Marlow, mate?'

'Aye, pass him aft here, Cap'n,' another voice called. 'We'll toss him over the side and gladly.'

'Ye'll toss nobody over the side, 'cept I tells ye to,' Bridger retorted, scowling at the group of men. 'Ye're sailing wi' Captain Sam Bridger now and I'll say what's to happen aboard this ship.'

Someone laughed and a cheer rose, the bearded, sun-tanned faces grinning.

'Sounds as bad as Marlow,' a man shouted.

There was laughter and Bridger nodded approval. Jacko was back beside the man, holding the lantern up and Matt could see how delighted the crew were to find themselves freed from Captain Marlow. They were slapping each other's backs, grinning and asking Bridger what was to happen now.

'What are ye going to do wi' Marlow and the mate . . . and that man-killing bosun?' a voice demanded. 'We owes them something, mate.'

'We'll drop 'em off somewhere tomorrow,' Bridger told them. 'Find an island and land 'em. Then we sails for New

Providence.' He heard the growl that greeted his words and scowled ferociously, lifting his pistols. 'Ye heard me, ye scruff,' he snarled. 'We'll do no killing unless we has to. And any one of ye that don't want to sail wi' me can land wi' Marlow. When we get to where we're bound, ye'll have a share of what the cargo fetches and that'll be more'n ye have earned in yer lives before. But if ye come wi' me ye'll be listed as pirates and if ye're ever found ye'll be hanged. Any of you who wants to stay with Marlow can go wi' him tomorrow, for I'll ask no man to risk his neck.'

'I'll sail wi' ye, Cap'n Bridger,' a man roared, 'and not the first time I've sailed under the black flag.'

Others took up the cry, but some were silent, looking apprehensive. But Bridger seemed satisfied. He grinned on the men.

'I'll have ye rich in a month,' he promised. 'And now we can drink to our luck. Who knows where the grog is stowed aboard this ship? We'll break out a keg and toast all jolly sea rovers and fat prizes.'

'It's wi' the steward, down aft,' a man shouted. 'But Marlow's got his own in his berth . . . the best brandy, Cap'n.'

Bridger turned, beckoning Matt with a swing of his arm.

'See what ye can find in Marlow's cabin, younker,' he ordered. 'Send the nigger out with what's there.'

Matt hurried across the quarterdeck and into the great cabin, to find a candle had been lit and stood on the long table. The Negro was on a stool, sitting near Captain Marlow's bed, where the shipmaster lay on his back. He had been secured with rope from his wrists and ankles, tied to the corners of the bed, so that he looked like someone being tortured on a rack. A piece of dirty cloth was tied round his face, forced into his mouth so tightly that the loose flesh of his cheeks bulged like small balloons. The man's eyes glared at Matt balefully, and even as the boy knew the shipmaster was helpless, he felt a cold shiver of fear down his spine.

'We've to find liquor,' Matt told the Negro.

They searched together, finding chests filled with clothes and charts, and one with leather bags that felt as though they contained money. Finally they found bottles and carried them to the deck, where Bridger grasped one by its neck and told Matt to pass round the others. He sent the Negro back for more, then grinned at the boy.

'Did ye have a look at Marlow?' he demanded. 'Is he offering to carry ye to yer uncle now, younker?'

'They've gagged him,' Matt answered. 'He'll choke the way they've done it. D'ye have to do that, sir?'

'Let him roar as much as he wants now,' the man said contemptuously. 'Take the gag off him if ye want to, lad.'

Matt went back to the cabin, meeting the Negro bringing more bottles. He stood beside the bed, watching the shipmaster nervously.

'I'll take your gag off, Captain Marlow,' he said. 'You'll not be harmed if you behave.'

He found where the cloth was knotted and untied it, avoiding the man's glaring eyes. Captain Marlow worked his jaws when the cloth was removed, watching the boy all the time.

'Ye'll be sorry ye ever got mixed up wi' this, boy,' he croaked thickly, 'and if ye're sensible ye'll cut me free and hand me that pistol ye're carrying.'

'You'd be shot before you left the cabin,' Matt told him, 'and also I do not want you to be free again. You deserve this for kidnapping me and Jacko.'

The man sneered.

'Ye'll wish ye had, when they're slipping a rope round yer neck,' he retorted threateningly. 'Getting mixed up wi' a mutiny!' He raised his head, peering towards the cabin door and listening to the noise going on outside. Men were laughing, shouting at someone and a voice roared from somewhere.

'Open this companion, ye murderous dogs,' the voice demanded, 'afore I break it down.'

B.J.—H

There was another roar of laughter, and voices jeered, taunting the mate inside the companion-way. Captain Marlow looked at the boy cunningly.

'That's the mate, boy,' he said softly. 'Ye jest cut me free and then go and unfasten them doors. Ye're a smart lad, and I'll see ye get to Virginia. You help me get the ship back and we'll have them rogues dangling afore they know what's come on them.'

Matt looked down indignantly.

'You are fortunate it is not you who is dangling now,' he said warningly. 'If Sam were not so good-natured you would be. The crew wanted to throw you overboard.'

'That scum,' the man spat contemptuously. 'If they was any good to man or beast they'd not be slaving for ten shillings a month. And that gaolbird, Bridger! He's no fit company for a lad like you, Matt. Nor that thieves' brat wi' him. They'll lead ye to the gallows, boy, when ye might be lording it in Williamsburg. Ye're mad to join in such as this.'

'I'll stay with them just the same,' Matt retorted, 'and reach Virginia. I wouldn't trust you an inch, Captain Marlow. You are more evil than Sam Bridger and deserve all that happens.'

A chuckle sounded behind the boy and he spun round, to find Bridger looming over him, grinning widely and with a bottle grasped in one hand, a pistol in the other.

'Now that's no compliment, Matt,' the sailor chided humorously, 'for this fat swab is ahead of me by miles when it comes to villainy. I never put human beings where he's put 'em, never sold men and women into slavery, and when I've robbed it's been clean honest plundering.' He looked down at the mountainous figure on the bed contemptuously. 'If I hadn't promised this lad I'd not slit yer throat, ye'd be lying there dead now,' he went on harshly. 'Or swimming for Barbados like the men ye've abused want. Open that foul mouth of yours again and that's what ye'll be doing.'

'If ye had the sense of a louse that's what ye would do,' Captain Marlow snarled defiantly, 'for ye'll live long enough to be sorry ye spared me. No man ever robbed Dan Marlow and got far wi' his plunder.'

Bridger laughed.

'A man, by all that's holy,' he exclaimed admiringly, 'and no sniveller. It's worth saving yer neck to hear ye.'

He spun round as a shot sounded, the explosion muffled and seeming to come from under the deck. There were cries of alarm, then yelling. Jacko appeared in the cabin doorway, his eyes bright with excitement and, to Matt's horror, one thin hand grasping a bottle.

'It's the mate, Sam,' the boy shouted, 'firing through the door. Want us to send a volley back at him?'

Bridger shook his head, smiling widely.

'I'm getting to like that little bully,' he said. 'Least him and Marlow ain't cowards. Leave him be, sprat.'

He strode to the doorway as the men on deck began to shout oaths and abuse at the defiant mate. Matt hurried after him, to find the quarterdeck crowded with already half-drunken seamen who were keeping well away from the companion-way but screaming towards it. Bridger thrust his pistol into his breeches and grasped one man by his long hair, flinging him against his mates.

'Get off this quarterdeck, ye scruff,' the *Avon Pride*'s new captain roared furiously. 'I'll cut down the last man I see aft of that hatch.'

He was obeyed with an alacrity that made Jacko chuckle and Matt smile, for the men ran from the tall threatening figure, to stand when he roared at them again.

'Now fling them bottles over the side,' he told them harshly. 'Ye've had all the drink ye'll see till we gets ashore. And I'll keel-haul the next man I hears abusing them they was scared to look at until somebody else clapped them below. . . . I got no love for Marlow or his mate, but at least they're men. We'll give them the respect due them who don't snivel, and when we send them ashore tomorrow I'll make anyone who insults them go wi' them.' He stood, feet apart and scowling, then gestured them forward. 'Now git back to yer corners,' he ordered, 'and don't come aft here again until I send for ye.'

The men obeyed with a meekness that startled Matt Tuke and made him gaze at Bridger admiringly. Jacko chuckled.

'A proper captain, eh, Matt?' he whispered hoarsely. 'He should ha' been an admiral or something.'

8

PIRATE STRONGHOLD

Sam Bridger kept his promise to send the dispossessed officers
away from their ship with what he considered to be fitting
ceremony. Early in the following afternoon, when the *Avon Pride*
had been sailing northward since dawn and the dark-green bulk
of the island of Hispaniola lay far astern, a group of small islands

were sighted and the ship was brought within half a mile of the smallest of these, a mere sand-bank with a few trees clustered on its summit. Sails were trimmed to hold the ship into the light wind and a boat was lowered to the water. Four men climbed into it, two to row and two armed with pistols and cutlasses. A small keg of fresh water was placed in the boat, with a half-sackful of hard ship's biscuits that would be all the food the marooned men would have unless they found something on the island. When Matt Tuke protested that these provisions would not sustain the five men who were being landed for more than a day or two, Bridger laughed and said Captain Marlow needed thinning down and it was very likely the shipmaster had marooned others with less.

Bridger had dressed himself for his role of ship's captain and for the ceremony he was planning. He had raided Captain Marlow's chests and that forenoon he appeared on deck wearing a long, dark-red, velvet coat and satin breeches, yellow silk stockings with soft leather shoes, lace frothing at his neck and cuffs, and with a silver-ornamented rapier-hilt showing above a long scabbard at his side. He had washed and shaved, and with his long reddish-brown hair drawn back and tied with a ribbon, he looked a handsome and impressive figure. Jacko whistled his admiration and Bridger grinned, thoroughly pleased with himself.

He ordered the crew aft to watch their old captain and his officers being sent away, warning them with threats to skin them alive if they uttered a word of abuse against Marlow, then he summoned the mate and his companions on deck.

'Ye can have yer daggers, but no other weapons,' he called into the companion-way, 'and leave yer gear. Come up and go over the side quiet and ye'll go unharmed.'

He stood back then, holding two pistols as the small, brown-faced mate appeared. He was followed by the ship's elderly carpenter and a white-faced man who was the steward. A growl came from the men gathered forward of the quarterdeck as the mate sneered and spat at Sam Bridger's feet.

'Keep them clothes ye've stole for a month,' the fiery little officer snarled, 'and they'll be yer shroud. I'll watch every man of ye swing for this.'

He turned then, and strode to the ship's side and climbed into the boat, his two companions following him quickly. They were followed by the huge bosun, recovered from the blow on his skull and now scowling but silent. When Captain Marlow appeared, followed by the Negro and Hardcastle, who had released him from his bonds, even Sam Bridger's threats could not silence the growl of hatred that came from the crew as they saw their taskmaster again. He ignored them, his eyes only for the splendidly apparelled Bridger, and his thick lips drew to a sneer as he recognized his own clothing. Bridger grinned, bowing and gesturing towards the ship's side.

'Yer boat's alongside, Cap'n Marlow,' he said with mocking politeness, 'an' I hopes we meet up again some time when ye've another cargo to give away.'

'We'll meet sooner'n ye think, ye thieving scoundrel,' Captain Marlow retorted. 'And my cargo will be hemp for yer neck.'

'Let's toss him over the side, Cap'n,' a man shouted, 'an' see if he can swim ashore.'

Bridger laughed.

'Ye heard that, Cap'n Marlow?' he said. 'Ye best go quickly afore they takes charge of ye.'

The shipmaster snorted, turning and striding towards the gangway opening in the bulwarks. Matt, standing near the companion canopy, moved back to conceal himself from his enemy, upset and nervous by what he was seeing. Captain Marlow saw the movement and looked towards the boy, then stopped, a threatening scowl on his slack-fleshed face.

'Aye,' he growled scornfully. 'Ye do well to hide yerself, boy. I blame you for this, for ye could have warned me of these rogues' plotting. I'll not forget it, and ye'll suffer wi' the rest of the scruff ye've sided wi'.'

'Leave the lad alone,' Sam Bridger called harshly. 'I've told ye before . . . if it wasn't for him ye'd not get even the chance ye're getting.'

Captain Marlow snorted again, but he could see the crew had moved closer to him and could hear their threats. He gave the boy a last fierce glance, then strode to the ship's side, holding himself defiantly to the last. In the boat he looked away from the ship that had been stolen from him, leaving the fiery little mate to spit back at the men who now lined the bulwark rail and yelled taunts at the dispossessed officers. The boat was pushed away from the ship's side and rowed towards the small island, and Matt climbed to the sterncastle to watch it. He saw it touch the sun-glistening white beach and the marooned men landing, the bosun and the steward carrying the meagre food supplies while Captain Marlow and the mate stood and watched the ship. Even from this distance, Captain Marlow seemed to threaten the boy, and Matt knew he would not feel safe until he was in Virginia and protected by his uncle. The shipmaster would never forgive nor cease to try and revenge himself on those who had robbed him, and Matt Tuke would be his most hated victim.

But Matt's fears were clearly not shared by the others aboard the *Avon Pride*. With the boat back alongside and lifted aboard, Sam Bridger's voice as he roared out the orders that brought the crew running to sheets and braces rang with a new assurance and authority, and the men responded cheerfully and with a will, as though getting rid of Captain Marlow had relieved everyone of fears they had, even while the shipmaster was secured and helpless. When Matt came from the poop after watching the tiny island and the five lonely-looking figures on the beach disappear astern, he found men who laughed and joked while they worked, Sam Bridger pacing the quarterdeck with all the aplomb of a real ship's captain and Jacko strutting proudly in a blue coat he had found among the mate's possessions, a cutlass dragging on the deck at his side and a large pistol thrust into his breeches. He greeted Matt with a proud grin.

'There's fine clothes a-plenty down below,' he told the boy. 'Ye can rig yerself proper, chum.'

'I'll stay as I am, Jacko,' Matt answered; 'I want only to get to Virginia.'

'An' ye will,' the other declared boastfully. 'Me an' Sam'll have ye there in no time.'

'You will come with me, Jacko?' Matt said sharply. 'Ye'll not stay with Sam?'

'And why not, chum?' Jacko demanded. 'I always fancied meself in satin an' velvet, and pirating seems the right way to get them. I'll not go back to gleaning for pennies while such sport can be found.'

'They hang you for piracy,' Matt warned and Jacko laughed.

'They hang ye for filing a drunken sailor's pocket,' he retorted. 'So best take what's biggest. The rope bites no tighter and the sport's better.'

He turned and swaggered away, joining a group of sailors who applauded his war-like appearance and told him he looked every inch a real sea rover. Sam Bridger roared, summoning the boy to him and ordering him to help the Negro scrub out the great cabin, and, as Jacko protested at such a task, cuffing him soundly.

'Ye're no passenger,' the man warned him. 'Ye're ship's boy now, and ye'll jump when I calls. Strip off them fancy trappings and get a bucket, afore I has ye ducked over the side for mutiny.'

The boy obeyed, scowling as he went, and Bridger grinned.

'You, Matt, take a hand along and break out that slob Bassett,' he ordered. 'Tell him he's officers'-mess man now and start him cleaning up below. Then go through Marlow's chests and see what's there. . . . Count what money's aboard and write out a list of the arms. Ye're the only one aboard who can count to ten. See if there's a list of the cargo. . . . Ye'll serve as captain's clerk while ye're here.'

The scar-faced sailor was quickly showing himself as a masterful commander who demanded immediate obedience and respect for the rank he had assumed. Even Jacko and Matt had to give him his title of 'Captain' and were allowed no familiarities, and any of the crew who had thought that the removal of Captain Marlow would mean a slackening of dicipline and an easier time were soon disillusioned. They learned that Bridger's huge fist could be even more painful than the red-headed bosun's and that Bridger drove them harder than the departed mate. As the *Avon Pride* sailed northward towards the island of New Providence, Matt marvelled more and more that men would suffer the treatment they got aboard a ship, and he wondered also why Bridger bullied so much. The sailor told him why, one day when he had knocked a man down for some small misdemeanour.

'Ye've got to drive trash like this lot,' Bridger said contemptuously. 'An' besides, I want them to get out of the ship when we reach New Providence. There ain't one among them would make a freebooter and I'll find a proper crew when we get there.'

Matt was spending much of his time with Bridger in the eight days' voyage, for only he, Hardcastle, and Bassett were able to read or write and Bridger distrusted both the men. He treated Bassett like a cur dog and the once stout little man, now reduced to a nervous wreck, kept out of his way. Hardcastle had been appointed ship's mate, though he had no knowledge of sea affairs, and his task was to watch the men and report any signs of mutiny or discontent, but Bridger kept the cargo lists and any knowledge of the money found in Captain Marlow's chests from him.

'You're the only honest one aboard, lad,' the sailor told Matt with good-humoured scorn. 'Even Jacko's got sticky fingers where money's concerned.'

Matt's employment made the voyage interesting and helped him to forget those five lonely figures left on the tiny island. Bridger liked to talk to the boy and Matt learned to admire the man more and more, even as he lamented his brutality to the men and his pride in being a sea robber. The sailor seemed to grow in stature now he commanded a ship, and even the men he drove so mercilessly admired his seaman's skill. He had not boasted when he had said he knew the West Indies and the Caribbean, for now he worked the *Avon Pride* between islands and through channels where the sea bottom seemed to rise almost to the ship's keel.

'I learned these waters from one of the best freebooters ever to take a prize,' the man said when Matt praised his knowledge, 'and when ye fly the jolly roger ye've got to know them. There's over two thousand islands and keys—sand-banks—in the Bahamas, and the channels between them are shallow and foul wi' coral reefs. That's what makes this a safe place for pirates, for men-o'-war captains dassent risk their ships where we sail. They need too much water and even the *Avon Pride* is too deep-keeled for working round here. When we go after plunder, I'll sail her north, along the North American coast, until I finds myself a shallow-drafted, fast-sailing schooner like pirates favour.'

He showed the boy how he chose the safe channels between the islands, by steering for landmarks he recognized and by the colour of the water. The water was so clear that looking down on it from aloft was like standing on the edge of a cliff and seeing the land below, and every underwater colour was visible from a long distance, the sea's surface becoming a vast pattern of blues, pinks, and yellows or the glittering reflection of the hot sunlight. Each colour told Bridger what lay below the surface, either sand-bank or coral growth, and how deep the water was. Matt, clinging to the rigging near the man, listened fascinated as Bridger pointed to where it was safe to sail the ship, then looked down to see the pale sands or wonderfully shaped and tinted coral where fish of every hue and size seemed to move in empty space. The boy watched shoals of tiny, brilliantly coloured fish with fins as large as a bird's wings flutter past, the dark, ugly shapes of gropers nosing close to the sand, the sinister, graceful sharks that followed the ship, and hump-backed turtles paddling desperately out of her way. For the time, the boy could forget he was aboard a ship stolen from her owner and with desperate sea robbers, and enjoy the perfect weather and thrill of Bridger's navigation among the lovely islands.

But the boy's pleasant holiday from anxiety ended when, eight days after Captain Marlow had been marooned, Bridger sailed the *Avon Pride* into the anchorage at New Providence. He brought her in with a flourish, knowing the strange ship was being watched by people ashore and from the decks of several lean black vessels already anchored off the pirate settlement. The anchorage was in front of the settlement, protected from the eastward by a long, narrow, tree-clustered island, and Bridger sailed the *Avon Pride* into the haven with every sail filled and the crew standing by to cast off ropes from their belaying-pins, others on the forecastle to drop the anchor when he gave the order.

There was a fresh breeze blowing from the east and the ship was moving at a full six knots when Bridger headed her for the anchorage. His crew waited, then watched apprehensively as the beach came closer and closer, the ship passing the anchored vessels, and no order came to bring her round into the wind. It seemed as though Bridger would drive her half-way up the gleaming sands, when his voice roared the order to 'Let go forrard'. As the anchor splashed into the water Bridger thundered at the men on the upper deck, and halyards, braces and other ropes were cast off their pins, gear tackles were let go and sails and yards came down with a rush, men leaping clear of the tumbling canvas and heavy spars. Bridger roaring at them to show what sort of sailors they were. The *Avon Pride* came to a sudden jerking stop, the men on the forecastle risking their limbs as they checked the thick anchor cable. She came round to it, masts shaking and the ship lying over, before rolling and quivering like a living thing. Bridger's laughter came ringing out as the startled crew recovered from their shock and cheered him. He grinned his delight, demanding that a boat be lowered to take him ashore, calling Matt to him.

'You'll come ashore wi' me, younker,' he ordered. 'Jacko, too. . . He'll find some proper rogues in New Providence.'

He went to the great cabin, to appear again carrying a bulging leather satchel. The boat was already in the water, two men at the oars, and Bridger shouted for Hardcastle.

'Ye'll see these swabs clear up this mess,' he said, gesturing to the tangle of canvas, ropes, and spars. 'Then let 'em come ashore. I'll be at the tavern, wi' Matt here being paymaster.'

Again the men cheered him, delighted by the prospect of being ashore and sharing in the plunder taken from Captain Marlow. Matt and Jacko climbed to the boat, Bridger leaping after them, and it was headed for the shore and towards a crowd which had gathered to see who this dashing newcomer was. Bridger stood up in the stern, scanning the faces of those on the beach, to suddenly roar a name and wave.

'Ahoy there, Black Tom,' he bellowed. 'D'ye not know an old shipmate when ye see him?'

'Sam Bridger!' a villainous-faced, bearded ruffian answered thunderously from the beach. 'I heard ye was hung.'

He came to the water's edge, to grasp at the boat's stern and drag it on to the sand.

'Should ha' known it was you,' he declared, admiringly. 'The way ye brought yer ship in.'

Bridger had climbed over the men rowing the boat and now he leapt to the beach, to be hugged by the bearded pirate and then introduced to others who came round, their eyes on the satchel he carried, as they pumped at his hand and slapped his broad shoulders. Bridger was clearly delighted, lifting and shaking the satchel so that the coins clinked, roaring for all hands to join him in the tavern. Matt and Jacko leapt from the boat, to be followed by the two seamen who had brought them ashore, the boat allowed to lie where it was or drift away. Jacko was smiling widely and nudged Matt with an elbow.

'Here's a rogue's den, chum,' he said hoarsely. 'I've not seen worse in Newgate itself. We'll have sport here.'

He grinned at a crowd of children who came round them, whining for pennies and holding out grimy hands. The children were black and white and every shade of brown, half naked, what clothes they wore ragged and soiled, and Matt was shocked by the hunger in their eyes. Jacko was tossing coins to them, laughing as he watched the children fight and scramble for the money. Women, some of them dressed in what had once been expensive finery, were running after the men, calling to Bridger, and he was laughing and handing out money to the hands stretched towards him. He roared for Matt and the boy ran to his side. Bridger thrust the satchel at him.

'Here, lad,' he said, 'you take charge of this. When we get into the tavern ye'll stand by to pay the hands as they come ashore. Give 'em five guineas a man. . . . Jacko! Stay with Matt and spit the first hand that reaches for the gold.'

They had reached the pirate settlement, a straggling, untidy cluster of miserable shacks built with driftwood, pieces of ships' timbers, logs and old canvas. The roofs were either canvas or palm branches, and round each miserable shanty was the filth and rubbish tossed out by people too lazy to carry it as far as the water. The huts were along the top of the beach, close against thick green jungle growth, though here and there clearings had been made among the trees and bushes. There were no roads, only paths among the tangle of ramshackle buildings. Bridger led the way towards one long, more solid building with a wooden sign-board over the doorway, where a stout man wearing a dirty apron waited to receive and fawn on this moneyed visitor. Bridger clapped a great hand on his shoulder, ordering him to roll out kegs of rum for the crowd to drink Sam Bridger's health. He thrust past the man, Matt close behind him, hugging the heavy satchel and Jacko snarling and threatening with his dagger anyone who came too near. Inside the smoke-filled, odorous tavern, Bridger flung coins on to a long bar made from roughly levelled planks, demanding liquor for all hands. Matt went to one of several tables in the room, Jacko standing behind him with dagger bared but watching the scene eagerly. The two seamen who had rowed them ashore came up grinning widely, and Matt gave them each five guineas, then watched them pushing through the crowd of pirates who had come into the tavern, making for the bar where the landlord and two slatterns were pouring every sort of drink

into leather and pewter tankards, and men were clamouring for their share.

So began an experience that Matt Tuke was never to forget, and which sent him out of the tavern hours later with his head aching and his stomach retching from the noise and the smell of tobacco smoke and drink. If the boy had ever believed pirates to be romantic characters, he was now thoroughly disillusioned, for he had seen men fighting like beasts, unable to speak without a flood of oaths, degrading themselves by fawning on Sam Bridger, and the men from the *Avon Pride* who became kings for an hour on the strength of the few guineas Matt gave them. Bridger was lord of them all, for he was flinging money out recklessly, demanding that men sing for their drinks, or dance when he ordered. He fired his pistols over the landlord's head when that perspiring rogue did not serve him quickly enough, and he flung a man who tried to pick his pocket through the doorway and among the swarm of children who shrieked and begged outside the tavern. Men fought for the sailor's bounty, struggling on the sandy ground that was the tavern's floor, Bridger urging them on with drunken glee.

Matt pushed out of the place as soon as the satchel was emptied, thrusting children aside as they grasped at him and begged for pennies. He almost ran down the beach, followed by screaming children, until he found a boat and pushed it afloat. He sculled to the *Avon Pride*, to find the deck deserted, and sat on the hatchway to recover from his experience. The man Hardcastle came from the great cabin, to watch the boy solemnly, then return inside the cabin. Matt went below, to the carpenter's cabin that he now shared with Jacko, finding the once plump Bassett seated in the mess room. The boy told him of what was happening ashore and Bassett nodded miserably.

'We are among thieves and murderers, boy,' he said despairingly, 'and are being punished for our errors.'

'I committed no errors,' Matt retorted indignantly, 'except in trusting those who betrayed me.'

'As I did, boy,' the man whined. 'I trusted the chemist when he said five grains would serve.'

The boy rose, disgusted by the man's words.

'You should have gone with Captain Marlow,' he said scornfully.

There were times in the next six weeks when Matt Tuke almost wished he had gone with Captain Marlow himself, or had accepted the shipmaster's offer to carry him to Virginia. For it seemed now he would never reach his uncle, nor escape from New Providence. He did not see either Sam Bridger or Jacko for the whole first week of the *Avon Pride*'s stay in the pirate harbour, and he lived lonely days in an almost deserted ship, with only the company of the whining, miserable Bassett, the lugubrious Hardcastle, and a steadily dwindling number of disgruntled sailors. Less than half the crew returned from their first night's carouse, and those who did come back looked pale and exhausted from their jollifications, some of them with cuts and bruises from brawling. They were all without money, complaining that Bridger had not shared out Captain Marlow's gold fairly and had kept most of it for himself. They wandered around the deck, or slept the days away, and then disappeared one by one. Two of them tried to load a boat with bales of cloth from the cargo, and Hardcastle caught them. He held pistols at them while they re-turned the bales to the hold, then ordered them ashore, with a warning that if they came near the ship again they would be shot. The ship herself became steadily dirtier and untidier, for no one attempted to wash down the decks or attend to her, and rubbish gathered against the bulwarks and where it was flung.

So it was an indignant Matt who watched Bridger and Jacko come aboard at the end of the first week, for the boy felt that he was being treated shabbily and that Bridger's promises meant nothing.

'You promised to get me to Virginia,' he accused hotly, 'and it looks like I will stay here for ever. I had done better to trust Captain Marlow.'

The man laughed, gripping the boy's shoulder in a comradel[y]
way.

'Ye'll be there, lad,' he promised, 'but we have to sell this carg[o]
first and I'll sooner burn it than take the prices offered by th[e]
rogues in this place. We wait for merchants to come fro[m]
America. Then we sail for there to land the cargo, for that is ho[w]
ye get fair prices.' He smiled his sympathy. 'There's no other wa[y]
to get to the colony, younker, so ye must have patience.'

'You make yourself miserable staying aboard the ship,' Jack[o]
broke in, 'and ye'd find sport enough and lively company if y[e]
come wi' me, chum.'

'Aye, an' end up with a cutlass in his belly,' Bridger remarke[d]
'as you and that gang of mohawks ye've gathered who a[re]
robbing the settlement right and left will end. If ye're caught ye'[ll]
find pirates are wors'en London magistrates when it comes t[o]
punishing thieves.'

But Jacko grinned his contempt for all pirates, winking t[o]
Matt, then swaggering away, ludicrous in his man's long coa[t,]
his trailing cutlass, and the pistols in his breeches. Sam shook h[is]
head.

'Did ye say ye'd make an honest lad out of that?' he aske[d]
Matt. 'He's gathered a wild pack ashore and no man wi' mone[y]
in his pocket is safe from them. I've had to save his neck twic[e]
already, but someone'll have him if he don't ease down on h[is]
tricks.'

Bridger was delighted to find only a few of the *Avon Pride*[']
crew remained aboard, for he had wanted to get rid of them an[d]
find a bolder lot of men. He gave those who remained a fe[w]
shillings, swearing it was all he had until the cargo was sold, the[n]
watched them hurry ashore to get what pleasure the money woul[d]
buy. When he saw Bassett he shook his head sorrowfully.

'We'll have to get rid of you, fatty,' he announced, 'afore y[e]
shrivel to skin and bone. . . . How'd ye like to sail aboard a shi[p]
that's looking for a crew?'

Bassett looked at the sailor helplessly.

'Do with me what you will, sir,' he whimpered. 'I am a lost soul and nothing matters.'

Bridger laughed, then went to the great cabin to find the last of Captain Marlow's money he had secreted there. He left the ship again, Jacko accompanying him, and Matt watched them go discontentedly. He felt helpless in this place and could only hope that Bridger spoke the truth and that merchants would come and buy the cargo and the *Avon Pride* would sail some time. That evening he watched Bassett leaving the ship and being carried to another, a low, black-painted schooner whose captain believed Sam Bridger when he said Bassett was the best ship's cook afloat. Matt watched the schooner leave the anchorage that night, admiring her grace and almost envious of Bassett. He, at least, was on the move, while the *Avon Pride* seemed stuck for ever. Matt would not have been envious if he had seen the schooner ten days later, beaten to a shattered wreck by the guns of a British warship, and with half her crew dead. Bassett was among the survivors who were landed in irons a few days after, to be bundled into carts and carried to Williamsburg. A crowd of people watched the pirates arrive at the public gaol in the Virginian capital, and as Bassett was dragged roughly from the cart by a guard a huge figure thrust through the crowd and ran towards him.

'Him!' Captain Marlow roared as he ran. 'He's mine. A damned mutineer who helped to steal my ship.'

It took four red-coated soldiers to hold back the irate ship-master, and when an officer arrived to demand what he wanted, Captain Marlow spluttered out his claim on Bassett. He was told he must appeal to Governor Alexander Spotswood, and the sailor pushed back into the crowd, to find a slim, sly-faced man whom Matt Tuke would have recognized.

'Come wi' me, Parker,' Captain Marlow commanded. 'I'll need ye to prove that he was one of my transported servants. Ye're known here as agent to Colonel Tuke and they'll believe ye when ye say ye saw that rogue in Bristol.'

'But I did not,' Parker protested. 'I saw four men being brought

to you as we left the inn, but it was dark then and I would recognize
none of them.'

'Ye'll still say ye saw him,' Captain Marlow retorted. 'Or
would ye sooner I called on Colonel Tuke to talk about his
nephew?'

This was the threat Captain Marlow had used on the clerk
since he had appeared in Williamsburg a month ago, and Parker
was helpless. He had been forced to introduce the sailor to
merchants who might need a captain for one of their vessels, and
to find money for his pocket.

'Everything I owned was in the *Avon Pride*,' Captain Marlow
had informed him, 'and when the man-o'-war picked us off that
island I made for here. Ye'll help me or ye'll hang . . . you and
that impostor ye're foisting on to Colonel Tuke. An' I'll get a
ship sailing out of Virginia where I can be handy when ye make
yer *coup*. 'Twas obliging you that lost me my ship, for without
that thieves' brat they call Jacko that ye landed on me, Bridger
would never have taken the ship. Ye owe me something and ye'll
start paying now.'

Parker dared not refuse, for he could be hanged for what he
had done, and also he was playing for high stakes. He was now
Colonel Tuke's agent in the capital, living comfortably and waiting
patiently for the day when the supposed Matt Tuke would
inherit his uncle's wealth. He had done as Captain Marlow demanded, and had worried over the fact that the real Matt Tuke
was free and might appear one day.

Now he accompanied the shipmaster to the Governor's new
palace, and assured a secretary that he knew Captain Marlow as an
honest trader who had been robbed and marooned, and that one
of those responsible was the man Bassett.

'You will have a pass to see this prisoner,' the secretary assured
Captain Marlow, 'and you can question him about your vessel.
Governor Spotswood is the relentless enemy of every pirate
afloat, as ye will know, and ye can count on his aid in anything ye
plan to get your ship back.'

Twenty-four hours later, Captain Marlow and Parker appeared before the Governor and the sailor told his story. The Governor listened, then glanced at Parker.

'That you have as witness a servant of my good friend, Colonel Tuke, assures me of your honesty, Captain,' he said. 'I'll do what I can to have this prisoner sold on your behalf . . . that is, if he can prove he was carried away against his wishes and is innocent of piracy. He must be tried with the others, however.'

'I ask ye for more than this, sir,' Captain Marlow demanded bluntly. 'I want yer help in getting my ship back. Bassett has told me that she still lies at New Providence, wi' her cargo untouched. The rogue, Bridger, hopes to find a merchant who'll give him a good price for the cargo and is waiting for some trader to visit New Providence.'

The Governor frowned.

'There is too much of this unlawful trade,' he said angrily. ''Tis our own officials and merchants who encourage these wretches by buying their plunder. I'd do much to stop such traffic.'

'And here's yer chance, sir,' Captain Marlow declared. 'Lend me a small craft and men to handle her, and we'll have that rogue bring the *Avon Pride* here to Virginia . . . to where ye'll have a reception awaiting him.' He turned, gesturing towards Parker. 'We'll send Master Parker wi' her, to offer a tempting price for the cargo and to arrange where it will be landed and when. 'Tis a chance for you to rid the seas of one pirate at least, and one who'll cause ye much trouble if he isn't taken soon.'

Parker rubbed his hands together nervously.

'Bridger might recognize me, Captain,' he protested, 'and if he doesn't the boys will. Ye'd best find someone else to act as trader.'

'Ye said yerself it was dark when ye passed the rogues,' Captain Marlow retorted, 'and ye needn't be seen, except by Bridger. Ye're quick-witted enough to find a reason for not showing yerself . . . break a leg, or say ye'd prefer not to be seen ashore. I want ye there, for I know no one smarter at handling such a business.'

'It seems an excellent plan,' Governor Spotswood interrupted 'and if Master Parker can tempt other pirates to these shores by offering high prices for their plunder, he'll be serving the colony and earning himself a substantial reward. If you attend here at thi time tomorrow, Captain, I'll have a naval officer discuss th matter with you and arrange where the ship has to come.'

He rose, announcing the end of the interview, and Captain Marlow took Parker's arm and led him from the room. Outside the clerk looked at the sailor worriedly.

'If I'm recognized ye lose yer ship for ever, Captain,' h pleaded, 'and ye know how dangerous that brat Jacko can be. advise ye to find someone else, for yer own sake.'

Captain Marlow chuckled, shaking his head.

'I'm sending you, Master Parker,' he answered. 'Ye'll act th part well and ye're cunning as a weasel. See no one but Bridger and never mind what the Governor wants of ye regarding othe rogues. 'Tis my ship and cargo we want back. . . .' He laughe at Parker's doleful expression and slapped a great hand on th clerk's thin shoulders. 'D'ye not see, we must be sure this plan i successful!' he cried. ' 'Tis not only my ship we want, but young Tuke. I'll be wi' those who take the *Avon Pride* when she come here and I'll see to it the lad never gets ashore. An' if he does, he'l hang with the others. . . . 'Tis time ye got rid of that danger fo ever, and this is the way to do it.'

9

THE LAST OF THE 'AVON PRIDE'

On a day two weeks after Captain Marlow's interview with
Governor Spotswood, Sam Bridger was rowed to a small ketch
that had arrived in the anchorage at New Providence the previous
evening, and whose captain, a quiet-spoken young man in
seaman's garb, had come ashore and announced that his vessel
carried an agent for Virginian merchants, who would be interested

in any merchandise being offered for sale. The agent could not come ashore, as he had suffered a broken leg when he was flung across the ketch's deck during a storm she encountered on the way to the Bahamas. Bridger was the third pirate to visit the ketch, the two others having returned ashore, to report delightedly on the prices they were to get for their plundered goods. They were to make up a cargo between them and deliver it to a place the agent had named and by a certain date.

Bridger was greeted by the young captain and taken below to meet the agent, a slender, narrow-faced man who sat on a long settee with his legs up and one in splints and bandages. He greeted the scar-faced sailor watchfully, inviting him to take a glass of sack, then examined the list of the *Avon Pride*'s cargo Bridger had brought.

'This is more to my liking,' the man said when he had read through the list. 'You have some excellent goods here, Captain.'

He began figuring with a crayon on a slate, then stated a price that brought a wide smile to Bridger's face.

'Ye'll have to think again, cully,' the sailor declared. 'I'd want twice what ye offer, and especially as ye'd require me to land the cargo in Virginia. That's a place where the likes of me is best clear of. I've heard of Governor Spotswood and his dislike of gentlemen of fortune.' He looked at the agent shrewdly. 'Ye take a great risk, landing such cargoes in Virginia, master,' he remarked.

The agent smiled thinly.

'I see I have a shrewd dealer on my hands, Captain,' he flattered. 'So state yer price and I'll meet it as close as my commission allows.' He met the other's eyes with a rueful smile. 'As ye say, Captain,' he confessed, 'we run some risk when trying to circumvent Governor Spotswood's cursed honesty. And 'tis because of his stand against such trade that those who employ me would offer more than ye'd get in Boston or New York. There the Queen's officers are more obliging, and wink an eye at such dealings as we do now, though one effect of this is that goods can be bought cheaper because they are easier landed. Because of

Spotswood's stand against merchants dealing with gentlemen such as yourself, merchandise is more expensive in Virginia than elsewhere in the colonies, and those London merchants who do trade with us ask high prices for the cargoes they send. Virginian merchants cannot see why they should suffer for the Governor's over-scrupulousness, and that is why I am come here on their behalf. I confess I had hoped to find more than I have, but your cargo will make the voyage worth-while if we come to an agreement.'

Bridger listened and chuckled to himself. He named a price, about half what the cargo would be worth if it had been honestly acquired, but much more than it would fetch in Boston or other American ports. The supposed agent whistled, but flattered the sailor with an admiring glance.

'I have to accept, Captain,' he said at last, 'or I return almost empty-handed. How quickly can you bring the cargo to us?'

'Three weeks from today,' Bridger answered. 'I have to gather a crew, and get the ship seaworthy. Where would ye have me come? Not too close to Yorktown or Hampton, master. Spotswood has got the Navy too damned alert round that coast.'

'If ye'll spread that chart at your elbow, I'll show ye,' the other said, and as Bridger unrolled the chart and held it flat on the table, the agent went on, 'Ye'll see an island—two islands, in fact—lying close to and just south of Cape Charles at the northern side of the entrance to Chesapeake Bay, Captain. Ye'll bring yer ship there . . . south of Fisherman Island, the larger of the two.'

Bridger was examing the chart and frowning. He could see where the agent described, and though he was relieved to find the rendezvous was a full fifteen miles from the dangerous Virginian coast inside Chesapeake Bay, he disliked the markings on the chart round the islands.

'A tricky place, master,' he said doubtfully, 'wi' shoal water all round. I'd need a pilot for these waters.'

'That's what makes the place suitable for our purpose,' the

other told him. 'Ye're well north of any ships entering or leaving
Chesapeake Bay. They keep south, close to Cape Henry where
there's deep water. If ye look close, ye'll see there's a channel
between the two islands, and once behind the smaller—the
Isaacs—ye lie snug and hidden. If ye approach from the sou'-west
wi' the dawn, a pilot will come off and bring ye in, and wi' yer
crew and the men I'll have there we'll have ye unloaded and gone
by nightfall.'

Bridger nodded approval.

'Ye have to get the goods to York River,' he said curiously.
'Do I discharge into another vessel?'

The other smiled.

'Again, that is why this place is so excellent,' he explained.
'We store the merchandise on the island, fetching it to York River
in small quantities wi' fishing boats. Then no one remarks on a
large amount of new goods appearing suddenly in the Williamsburg shops, wi' no record of their coming by ship. This has been
well plotted, Captain.'

'That I can see,' Bridger agreed admiringly. 'I had guessed ye
to be a smart rogue, master agent.'

They both laughed and the agent pointed to the wine
bottle. As they drank, Bridger looked at the agent good-
naturedly.

'Ye'll have the payment aboard when I arrive, sir,' he said,
'and I'd best warn ye against treachery. I'll have men standing by
their weapons until I leave ye, and they'll be the fiercest scoundrels
I can find in this den.'

'Ye need have no fears, Captain,' the other said hastily. 'Those
I act for do their pirating ashore.'

Bridger laid his glass down and took up his hat, the other
offering a slim hand. When the sailor returned to the ketch's deck
he was escorted to his boat by the young captain, noticing as he
went that the few seamen the craft carried were preparing her for
sea. As he was rowed towards the *Avon Pride*, the scar-faced
sailor was smiling widely, delighted with his skill as a bargainer

and with the way he had handled the agent. He climbed aboard his ship, to be greeted by an eager Matt Tuke and Jacko. He clapped a hand on Matt's shoulder.

'Ye'll be wi' yer uncle in three weeks from now, younker,' he announced. 'We sail for Virginia soon's I gather a crew and get the *Avon Pride* shipshape.'

'Was the ketch from Virginia?' Matt cried. 'Did you ask if they knew my uncle, and if Parker and my cousin were in Williamsburg?'

'Damme!' the man exclaimed. 'Never gave ye a thought, younker. I was too busy bargaining wi' that foxy agent.' He looked apologetic. 'Might have fixed for ye to sail wi' her if I'd thought,' he went on contritely. He swung round to look where the ketch had been anchored, and uttered an oath when he saw the small vessel was already under way, her sails filled and masts tilted as she headed away from the anchorage.

'They waste no time in getting out of here,' he said. 'Never mind, lad. Ye'll sail more comfortable aboard the *Avon Pride*, and 'tis only another few weeks and ye'll be giving yer cousin and Parker the shock of their lives.'

It was almost a month from that day before the *Avon Pride* reached the entrance to Chesapeake Bay and Matt could see the end of his wanderings. Weeks of neglect had done the ship no good and now she had to be made seaworthy again. She was hauled to the beach and tilted over, so that her new crew and men Bridger gathered from the settlement could scrape away a thick growth of barnacles and sea grass from her bottom, then smear the timber with tallow. Her sails, left stowed untidily and exposed to the weather, had to be unbent and taken ashore to be examined. Weakened canvas and rotted seams were repaired, and while this was being done other men overhauled every part of her rigging. Finally, she was armed for her new career of pillage. Extra cannon were brought aboard and set up against her bulwarks, kegs of gunpowder were stowed in the brick magazine at the after end of her lower hold, iron shot piled among the cargo, and bundles of

small arms—muskets, cutlasses and pikes—were packed in the
great cabin where they would be under Bridger's eyes.

At last she sailed, her new crew of forty desperadoes, not yet
sober after a final carouse, cheering from her deck and rigging,
while half-shotted cannon were fired off as a salute to the settlement. Sam Bridger, resplendent in another of Captain Marlow's
fine coats, conned the ship out of the anchorage and headed her
northward, abusing his crew good-naturedly and thoroughly
happy. Jacko, standing with Matt on the quarterdeck, gazed
towards the shore and the untidy jumble of shacks.

'That's what I call a proper place, chum,' he said regretfully.'I
feels at home there. There ain't an honest man in the place and ye
need all yer wits when ye go picking. If ye were going to live in a
place like New Providence, mate, I'd come wi' ye like a shot.'

Matt did not argue with the dark-haired boy. They had seen
little of each other in the past weeks, for Jacko was always ashore,
roving the settlement with a gang of young rapscallions, admired
by them for his trickery. That Jacko got a thrill from pitting his
wits and thieving skill against his victims Matt now accepted, and
he realized that they would part when the ship reached Virginia.
To put Jacko into a home and confine him to a regular employment would be like caging a wild creature. As Sam Bridger had
said, the boy was out of the city jungles and he would be unhappy
anywhere else. He was even bored at sea, for ship life gave no
scope for his restlessness and need for a challenge.

'What will you do, Jacko?' Matt asked a few days later, when
the other boy complained that sailing over seemingly endless water
was a sad way to live.

'Why, mate,' Jacko retorted, 'I'll go ashore in one of them places
like New York. I misses the smoke, chum . . . I like a stink in
my nose and feeling people round me. There's too much space
round ye at sea and there ain't nowhere to go.'

So Matt made no more effort to coax Jacko ashore and to
Williamsburg. He would miss the queer, restless boy, but
Bridger had been right. They were different sorts of people, drawn

together by accident and the affection that had come between them. Matt felt saddened by the thought of losing the other boy, but he knew now this had to be.

'I'll come and see ye, chum,' Jacko told him with sly humour, 'when ye're a rich planter and worth the robbing.'

The moment of parting seemed very close when the *Avon Pride* arrived off Cape Charles at the northern side of the entrance to Chesapeake Bay ten days after she had sailed from New Providence. Matt came on deck to find the ship moving slowly over an almost calm sea, and the rising sun lighting and colouring the water and exposing high green land some two miles away on the starboard side. Bridger had kept the *Avon Pride* out from the land all the voyage, not wanting to meet any warships which might be searching for pirates. Now he was bringing her in, men posted at each masthead to report any ships that appeared. The crew, Matt noticed, were armed, canvas-packed gunpowder charges and iron shot stacked handy to the cannon, pikes lying on the hatch covers. Sam Bridger was taking no chances of this being a trap, and now he was on the sterncastle, searching along the shores with a telescope. Matt joined him there and Bridger grinned.

'Ye'll soon be there, Matt,' he greeted, 'if that foxy-faced rogue keeps his word.'

A look-out hailed then, pointing, and Bridger aimed his telescope at a small boat that had appeared from the land and was being rowed towards the ship. He called to the deck, men adjusting the sails as the wheel was turned and the *Avon Pride* came to starboard, heading for the boat. As it came near Bridger grunted, recognizing one of the rowers as the captain of the agent's ketch. He descended to the quarterdeck, to greet the young man as he came over the bulwarks, the newcomer's eyes glancing along the deck at the warlike preparations. But he was smiling when he met Bridger.

'Ye made it, Captain,' he said. 'We've been watching for ye for a week.'

'Had to do work on the ship,' Bridger told him, 'and found light winds all the way. Hardly made four knots.' He looked at the young man suspiciously. 'Where's that agent wi' the money?'

The other man appeared surprised.

'He's waiting on the island,' he answered. 'Ye wouldn't expect him to come out here with money?'

Bridger scowled.

'I told him nothing goes out of this ship until I have the money,' he retorted. He paused, to look towards the land. 'I don't like this place, mate,' he said. 'Where's the anchorage?'

The other pointed towards the land.

'That's Fisherman Island, where the trees are lower than on the mainland beyond,' he explained. 'You can't make it out clearly against the cape. If ye put your glass to where I point ye'll see the channel between it and the Isaacs. Yer anchorage is in there and at the mouth of a creek on Fisherman Island, where ye'll lie snug and hidden from any vessel passing.'

Bridger had his telescope aimed at the land, and he could see where the other pointed to a narrow waterway between the southern tip of the larger island and a small treeless hump that was the Isaacs.

'A tricky place,' the scar-faced sailor said suspiciously. 'I've half a mind to swing about and get from here. I never trusted that foxy rogue.'

'That is your affair, Captain,' the young man answered, as though little interested in Sam Bridger's worries. 'I'm here to pilot ye and know nothing of yer trading. If ye don't want me, say so and I'll call my boat back.'

The young man's words and manner removed some of Bridger's suspicions, but he was still far from happy. He glowered at the island, then uttered an oath.

'Take her in,' he said roughly. 'If this is some sort of trick being played to get my cargo, whoever is doing it will wish they had played honest. There's forty men spoiling for a fight aboard here and they'll be ready for what comes.'

The young man laughed as though Bridger had made an excellent joke, then went to the ship's side and called to the solitary man in the boat.

'We'll go in now,' he sang out. 'You get back as fast as ye can.'

The boatman pushed away, to stand up and fit a short mast into its place then hoist a lug sail now the boat was going with the wind. The young pilot climbed half-way into the main shrouds, to stand on a ratline and con the ship. Sam Bridger, still uneasy and suspicious, climbed to the sterncastle from where he could see all round the ship. He looked seaward and to the south, for any ship that might be a warship, but the now sun-burnished water was empty. Bridger turned his telescope to the land ahead, seeing the channel clearly now as a narrow waterway between the tree-covered Fisherman Island on the ship's port hand and the small bare hump that was the Isaacs. The scar-faced man shook his head, frowning as he realized that once inside that channel the ship could not be turned and if this were a trap there would be little chance of escape, except by fighting.

'I dislike this place more every moment,' the man remarked to Matt as the boy stood near him. 'I have a feeling in my bones that we are being tricked.'

Matt laughed, too pleased by the thought of reaching his uncle to believe there would be more obstacles.

'Why should you think so, Sam?' he asked. 'Is it not usual to make such deals with merchants?'

'Aye,' the man agreed, 'but not Virginian merchants.' He was watching the island, and now he shrugged his shoulders. 'Maybe I am over-careful, younker,' he said. 'Ye get so when ye live as I have. The place seems harmless enough, and there's nowhere here for another ship to conceal herself.'

The young pilot called from his perch in the rigging.

'The anchorage is half-way through the channel, Cap'n,' he said, pointing towards the larger island, 'at the entrance to the creek. If ye'll have yer hands stand by the anchor, I'll sing out when to let go.'

Bridger climbed from the sterncastle, to summon the *Avon Pride*'s new mate, a stockily-built ruffian who listened to his orders, then led a dozen men forward to the forecastle. Topmen, the younger pirates, climbed aloft by the ratlines, while others stood by on deck to work the sails and cast off halyards and other ropes when the orders came to furl the sails. The ship was now close to the two islands and her lower sails were losing the wind. The heavy yards jerked as the canvas emptied and slapped loudly, and Bridger roared for these sails to be furled. Sheets and braces were cast off their belaying-pins, bunt-lines hauled on to gather the canvas to the yards, and the young topmen secured the sails to the yard in a rough stow. The *Avon Pride* went ahead slowly, to the wind in her upper sails.

Matt had remained on the sterncastle, standing against the waist-high hand-rail along the forward end of this higher deck. He could see down on to the upper deck, where men were coiling ropes on their belaying-pins and waiting to furl the topsails. Sam Bridger was standing near the wheel, watching his ship being controlled by the young pilot, frowning as he glanced at the near-by shores. Jacko was near the man, wearing, like Matt, only breeches and shirt with his shoes and stockings. He still carried a cutlass slung at his side, and a pistol at his waist. As though sensing Matt's presence, the boy looked up. He winked.

'Dinner wi' yer uncle tomorrow, chum,' he called and Matt nodded, smiling.

The *Avon Pride* was now entering the narrow channel between the two islands, their shores coming within a stone's throw of her sides. Matt left where he had been standing, to go farther aft and climb into the rigging of the ship's third mast, a short mizzenmast coming up through the sterncastle deck, carrying a small triangular sail that had already been gathered to its slanting yard. The boy climbed some ten feet above the deck, to settle himself on the ratlines. From this perch he could see along the ship's side and along her deck, to where the mate and his dozen men had laid out anchor cable and were waiting to let the anchor go from where it hung outside the bows from the cat-head beam. The young pilot was in the main rigging, facing forward, and Matt looked towards Fisherman Island. There the trees clustered thickly to the water's edge and Matt could see birds lifting from among the branches as they were disturbed by the ship. She was now moving slowly, a faint rippling from along her sides, and she seemed very close to the shore. The boy looked ahead, to see a break in the trees and what must be the entrance to the creek where the *Avon Pride* would anchor. She was almost there and Matt glanced at the pilot expectantly, waiting for him to warn Bridger. The young man did not sing out, then the ship was at the creek and Matt could see into it, a narrow waterway at right angles to the one the ship was in, like a tunnel, and seeming to penetrate far into the island.

Suddenly the pilot shouted, calling for the anchor to be let go and the men on the forecastle head obeyed. There was a loud splash and Sam Bridger was roaring angrily, furious that the pilot had not warned him they were to anchor. The ship was swinging to starboard, her stern coming round to port as the anchor held her bows. Matt exclaimed in alarm, seeing how close the stern was to the trees at the entrance to the creek. Bridger was yelling for the mate to check the anchor cable and prevent the ship coming astern, men were casting off ropes and hauling on leech-lines to gather the upper sails to their yards, topmen along the yards were clawing at the beating canvas and for the moment the upper deck was a scene of confusion and shouting. Matt did not see the pilot scramble to the deck and run aft to the ladder leading upward to the sterncastle, for the boy was watching the stern. He gasped with relief when he saw it come away from the trees, swinging into the creek and clear. Then he saw the first boat come from behind a small promotory and the sunlight glittered against metal. A second boat appeared, the oars working fast as men lay back, and Matt saw the red coats of the soldiers. He screamed a warning and as though this were a signal musket-fire burst from among the trees and shot came flying towards the *Avon Pride*. More boats had appeared, a fleet of them, each filled with soldiers. One of the young topmen on a yard screamed and fell, and from directly beneath Matt a voice sang out powerfully:

'Yield in the Queen's name. I am a naval officer and call on you to surrender!'

Matt stared down, to see the young pilot on the deck ten feet below, his arm raised and a pistol in his hand, pointing at Sam Bridger where he stood on the quarterdeck. The boy saw Bridger's face twist into a snarl of fury, saw him tugging at the pistol at his belt, and the pilot bring his weapon down to fire. With a scream of desperation, Matt leapt, landing on the pilot's shoulder as the pistol exploded, the man falling across the thick hand-rail from the impact. He gasped and uttered an oath, trying to twist round and grasp the boy who now clung to him with arms and legs, screaming wildly. Matt wrapped his arms round the man's neck and the pilot came upright, staggering backward, to crash into the high bulwarks, bringing a gasp of pain from the boy. His arms slackened and the pilot twisted round, to grip Matt at the waist and heave upward, lifting the boy and sending him flying over the bulwark. He saw the water under him and twisted to come down in an awkward dive and go under, swallowing water and striking out desperately. He came to the surface, gasping, to hear the yells and screams, the rattle of musket-fire and Sam Bridger's voice roaring for his men to repel boarders. The creek seemed to be filled with boats, soldiers firing from them as others fired from among the trees. The attackers had reached the ship's sides and were thrusting up at the pirates who leaned over the bulwarks to stab and slash downward. Matt saw a red-coated soldier fall from where he had climbed to the chain-wales, thick timbers projecting from the ship's sides, to which her shrouds were secured. A pirate shrieked and toppled into the water, cutlass blades clashed against pikes and swords, and Matt could look no longer. He turned and swam towards the nearest shore, to crawl from the water on to a grassy bank and lie there gasping and sobbing.

'Here's one of the rogues,' a voice exclaimed and a hand grasped Matt's shirt behind his neck and jerked him to a sitting position.

'Damme, a chit of a boy,' his captor exclaimed.

'Never mind him now,' another voice ordered. 'Keep your musket busy. These rogues out there are fighting like tigers and our lads have a task on their hands. We'll give 'em what aid we can.'

Muskets were being fired all round Matt and he raised his head, to see soldiers among the trees. He looked towards the ship, to see the battle still raging along her sides and the attackers being held off there. Invaders had got aboard at the ship's ends, however, and men were fighting on the forecastle and sterncastle, cutlasses flashing and pikes being thrust while shots flew from the shore and the boats. The boy could see bodies hanging over the *Avon Pride*'s bulwarks and lying on her deck, others floating in the water round her, and he knew the slaughter was heavy. He searched along the figures stabbing and slashing from the ship's sides, seeking Jacko and Sam Bridger, and he saw the man, standing on top of the bulwark near the mainmast, one hand grasping the shrouds as he stabbed down at the soldiers trying to climb aboard. But he could not see Jacko, and his heart was saddened as he thought of the boy being dead.

'They're being driven back,' a man exclaimed. 'Our lads have cleared the forecastle and are fighting on the upper deck.'

A cheer rose, and then Matt saw Jacko. Bridger had turned from the battle, holding to a shroud and reaching down inside the ship. Now he straightened, grasping a small figure by the back of its breeches. It was Jacko, his arms and legs jerking as Bridger swung him up and then outward. Matt cried in horror as the small form went through the air, above the boats, and into the water.

'The demons!' someone shouted. 'They've fired the ship.'

Smoke was rising from the *Avon Pride*, swelling out of her hold in a thick black pillar and Matt could see Bridger laughing and roaring, though the boy could not hear any words. But whatever Bridger was shouting it was having an effect. Men were scrambling over the bulwarks and dropping into the water, others raced along her deck to climb over the forecastle and leap from her bows, pirates and soldiers together in what seemed like a panic-stricken rush to get out of the ship. The battle had been abandoned, the ship was being deserted, and now only Sam Bridger remained, still on top of the bulwarks and laughing. Flames shot up, cutting through the cloud of smoke and seeming to leap at the sails and rigging, setting them alight like huge torches. The boats that had been alongside were being pushed clear, oars shipped and men rowing frantically towards the shore. Men were shouting, gesturing to other boats to get away, the soldiers who had been firing from the shore coming to the water's edge to ask what was happening. One of them shouted to a boat that had come near and a voice roared back.

'They fired her, near the magazine . . . ! She's going up in a minute.'

Matt looked towards the *Avon Pride*, now almost hidden by thick smoke and aflame everywhere. Bridger was still on the bulwarks, but even as the boy watched the man flung his cutlass into the water and leapt. His head appeared and Matt breathed easier, for Bridger was swimming strongly, overtaking others in the water. Boats were heading for the shore, though several with bolder crews were saving men in the water. Then the explosion came, deafening the ears and sending a rush of air that shook the tree branches. The *Avon Pride*'s rounded side bulged outward, her mainmast rose and hung like a huge torch before falling and crashing on to what was left of the ship. The sky was full of objects, shattered planks and flaming canvas and rope, that hung for a moment, then showered down on the water. The ship, her masts gone and fire burning along her decks, rolled over, sending up a cloud of grey smoke as the fires were extinguished. Then her bottom rose, water pouring from it, and a queer sound like a giant sigh came over the creek. The sound passed and there was silence, a hushing of all sounds, until a man's voice screamed, attracting every eye to a boat where a huge figure stood, arms above its head and fists shaking.

'My ship!' Captain Marlow was screaming. 'My ship!'

Someone behind Matt laughed harshly.

'And serve ye right, ye slob,' a soldier cried. 'If it wasn't for you getting the Governor to promise she'd be taken by boarding we could have had guns here and blown her and the foul pirates out of the water. Ye've cost good men's lives today and 'tis a pity ye haven't gone with yer ship.'

A hand gripped Matt's shoulder.

'Up younker,' the soldier who had grasped the boy said, not unkindly. 'We'll take ye where yer mates will be. . . . What's left of them.'

Matt rose, dazed by what had happened and shocked by seeing Captain Marlow. He stumbled beside the soldier as the man walked among the trees.

10

SENTENCED TO DIE

The woods seemed to have filled with men, uniformed soldiers and sailors who appeared among the trees. Now and then Matt saw water-soaked and scowling prisoners being driven in front of their captors, and occasional musket-shots sounded where pirates who had reached the island and were trying to escape had been discovered. The creek was visible through the woodland and boats were on the water, picking up soldiers and pirates where they clung to pieces of the wrecked ship. The *Avon Pride*'s bottom still showed above the surface, several men who had climbed there hailing the rescuers. Matt was only worried by thoughts of Jacko and Sam Bridger, and by the shock of seeing Captain Marlow. The shipmaster's appearance frightened the boy, even now when Williamsburg and the protection of his uncle was so near. This disaster had been of Captain Marlow's making, the result of his plotting to bring the *Avon Pride* to the island, and it seemed to the boy that the shipmaster could accomplish his revenge on all of them even now. He would be doubly vindictive after the loss of his ship, and would do everything he could to punish those who had robbed him, Matt Tuke among them.

'Here ye are, younker,' the soldier at his side said suddenly. 'There's what's left of yer mates.'

He pushed the boy into a clearing among the trees, towards where a dozen men squatting on the grass were guarded by soldiers. Other soldiers were in the clearing, some wounded and lying on the ground, others gathering round two fires near a small beach. As Matt was escorted to where the prisoners sat, Sam Bridger's tall form rose from among them and his voice rang out jubilantly.

'Matt, lad,' the sailor roared. 'Ye're alive.'

He stepped over the seated pirates and came towards the boy, to be halted by a soldier's pike and to stand grinning his delight. A smaller figure was leaping from among the prisoners, to dodge under the pike and Jacko flung himself at Matt, thin arms hugging and dark eyes joyful.

'Chum,' the familiar throaty voice cried, 'we thought ye was a goner. Saw that flammer toss ye over the side.'

Bridger reached out, drawing both boys into his arms and hugging them, chuckling and laughing.

'Ye saved me being shot by that swab, younker,' he said, gripping the boy's shoulder. 'I ain't forgetting that.'

A soldier was prodding at them with the butt of his pike, pushing them towards the seated pirates, but Matt was too happy in finding Jacko to notice the indignity. The smaller boy was watching him as though he would eat him, then he laughed throatily.

'Chum,' he whispered, ' 'twas me set the ship afire. . . . Tossed torches into the hold. Soon's we saw they was too many for us, Sam says we'll not let Marlow have her back and I gets torches and lights them. 'Twas that lump of lard that got us here . . . him and Parker.'

'He'll hate you and Sam worse than ever,' Matt exclaimed, looking at the boy worriedly.

'They'll hang us anyhow, mate,' Bridger retorted, 'and Marlow can't add to that. Governor Spotswood don't hand out the Queen's Pardon like some, and he thinks the only good pirate is a dead 'un.' The man smiled widely, a reckless gleam in his eyes. 'He'll see how a bold sea rover dies,' he boasted.

'Hold yer jaw,' Jacko burst out angrily, seeing the horror in Matt's face. 'Can ye see ye're upsetting my mate? We ain't hung yet, by a long chalk.'

'Matt's safe enough,' the man answered. 'When we gets to Williamsburg his uncle'll get him out of trouble. No need for him to be upset.'

'That's them!' a voice roared from behind Matt, and the boy swung round to see the huge figure of Captain Marlow a dozen feet away, a tall, red-coated army officer beside him.

The shipmaster was glaring at the two boys and Bridger, his slack cheeks quivering with rage and hatred. He pointed a thick finger at Bridger.

'There's the scum took my ship,' he screamed, 'wi' the two scruff who helped him. Ye should secure 'em well, Major, for ye've got a slippery handful.'

Sam Bridger was laughing, punching a fist into the other palm.

'My old shipmate, Cap'n Marlow,' he shouted as though delighted. 'Ye was right, jelly-belly. . . . We should ha' slung ye aloft like the hands wanted.'

'Aye,' the shipmaster snarled, 'an' I warned ye at the time. Now 'tis I who'll watch ye swing.' He glowered at the two boys, his eyes gloating on them. 'And yer two weasels, who helped ye. Yer age won't save ye where Governor Spotswood has the say.'

Matt met the man's spiteful eyes scornfully, then turned to face the army officer.

'Sir,' he said with what composure he could gather, 'I was kidnapped out of England by that man—I and Jacko. He is a spiriter and shares a plot to ruin me. My name is Matthew Tuke and my uncle is Colonel Tuke, whom you will know of.'

The boy held himself proudly, waiting for the officer to respond to his speech. But the officer looked more surprised than impressed, and Captain Marlow's mouth opened as though he were shocked to speechlessness. Then he laughed, a loud explosion of sound that brought the guards' heads round and caused the officer to look at the shipmaster in surprise. Captain Marlow's hands went to his vast stomach, gripping there as though his laughter hurt, his head shaking and his eyes admiring as he gazed on the boy.

'Damme!' he roared, slapping a thick hand on his thigh. 'He's still at it!' The loose cheeks shook as the man seemed to quiver in mountainous glee. 'That's yer best yarn so far, ye young swab. Ye'r Colonel Tuke's nephew, are ye now? Ye was a duke's heir when I shipped ye in Bristol.'

Matt gasped, too astounded to answer. He heard Sam Bridger utter an oath and Jacko made a low hissing sound. Captain Marlow was chuckling, watching Matt as though something in the boy delighted him.

'Ye hear him, Major?' the man demanded. 'He's Colonel Tuke's nephew now. He'll be the Governor's son next.'

'I do not understand, Captain,' the officer said, looking at the boy distastefully. 'Colonel Tuke has his nephew at college in Williamsburg.'

'That I know,' the shipmaster agreed, a chuckle rumbling from his throat, 'and that's where he could ha' got the yarn. Young Tuke an' the Colonel's agent, Master Parker, picked this young scrag up on the road from Exeter, when they were making for Bristol to sail for Virginia. He was being whipped out of a town and they takes pity on him and brings him to me, Parker knowing I was always willing to help an honest lad.' The speaker paused, to shake his head regretfully. 'I gives him a berth and finds out he's the biggest liar afloat. Tells me a yarn of being well-born and running away from home to find adventures. I did not believe a word he spoke, Major, but I needed a lad and didn't suspect I was shipping a treacherous young rogue.' He scowled on the boy. ' 'Twas him passed files to that mutineer.'

'What of me, Captain Marlow?' Jacko demanded, sounding as though he was admiring the man's invention. 'Did ye ship me out of yer good nature?'

Captain Marlow almost spat his hatred.

'Ye know well enough where you came from,' he snarled. 'From Newgate, wi' the other rogues.' He turned to the officer. 'Ye need no second look to tell what this young dodger is, Major,' he said contemptuously. 'Saved from the rope because of being a brat and sent aboard my ship for transportation to Barbados. Ye know what I told the Governor, and what was upheld by the rogue Bassett when he was questioned. There were two others, a nigger and a counterfeiter . . . and that pirate. He pointed at Sam Bridger and the scar-faced sailor laughed.

'So ye got that poor devil Bassett,' he said, 'and primed him to tell yer lies. Ye're a poor swab, Marlow; working yer spite against a lad who saved yer neck.'

'Who passed you files and helped ye take my ship,' the other snarled. ' 'Tis him I blame most for her loss and he'll suffer wi' the rest of ye.'

'He is lying, sir,' Matt cried, recovering from the shock of hearing Marlow's story. 'I am Matthew Tuke and the boy who is with my uncle is Peter Burdell, my cousin.'

'Ye'll have proof of this?' the officer asked scornfully. 'Looking at ye I'd say Colonel Tuke would not be flattered by your claim.' He turned, calling a soldier forward. 'Ye'll have these three taken apart and secured,' he ordered. 'It would seem they are the ring-leaders of this affair.'

The officer turned, and strode away, and Captain Marlow surveyed the two boys and Bridger with cruel satisfaction.

He leant towards Matt, leering at the boy. 'Yer name is Gubbins, lad,' he whispered vidictively. 'Least, so I had ye entered in my ship's articles. 'Tis a pity yer mates blew her up, or ye might have proved me a liar. Keep it in yer memory, lad. . . . 'Tis the name they'll hang ye wi' . . . Henry Gubbins.'

It was in this name, three weeks later, that Matt Tuke was sentenced to death by hanging, and by then the boy could only call on all his courage to accept and face his terrible fate. That he could turn away from the pitiless face of the Attorney-General of the Colony of Virginia to look on the handsome features of his uncle, seated with other splendidly dressed gentlemen in the public seats of the small court-room, was no consolation to the boy and would only have increased his distress. He stood as erect as he could between Sam Bridger and Jacko, his head held high, staring at the crown-surmounted, gilded insignia of royalty above the high-backed bench where his judge sat, thinking bitterly of these past weeks as the cold voice droned on.

'For one so young in years, Henry Gubbins,' the Attorney-General was saying, eyes peering from under a high, white wig, 'you have become old in sin. You have sought to escape the punishment of your crimes by lies of the most foolish invention. Not content with having aided other scoundrels in the stealing of a ship, the *Avon Pride*, and in having helped to cause the death of brave men when resisting the Queen's officers, you have caused pain, and, indeed, harmed the health of one—no older than yourself—who had befriended you in England. You have caused anxiety for a beloved nephew to one who is a highly honoured resident in this colony, persisting in this nonsensical claim even in this court-room. . . .'

Matt heard the judge's voice, like a rasp against his thoughts. He glanced down to where black-gowned and wigged lawyers were seated under the dais, watching a thick beam of sunlight that came through a round window opposite the deck where he stood with Sam Bridger and Jacko, their arms pinioned behind their backs. The sunlight touched and was reflected by the blade of a three-foot long silver oar placed in front of the judge, the symbol of an Admiralty Court, part of this cruelly emotionless ceremony that had worn Matt to a state of numb resignation. He hardly knew what the judge was saying, but Jacko must have believed he was suffering, for he pressed himself against Matt as though to comfort him and Sam Bridger winked to the boy encouragingly.

'They always like to hear themselves talking, younker,' he whispered. 'It's what they get paid for.'

The cold voice went on, listing Matt's crimes, but the boy was thinking of his uncle and how the planter had rejected him, so that now it did not matter what the judge called him. Colonel Tuke had come to see the boy at the gaol, curious about this young pirate who had demanded to see him and who claimed to be his nephew, Matthew Tuke. Parker had told the planter how he and Matthew—the Matthew who was now at the mansion twenty miles out of Williamsburg—had saved this young rogue from a public whipping and thought to help him by getting Captain Marlow to engage him as cabin-boy. And how Matthew and his cousin Peter had become fond of the ragamuffin, talking about their home and Peter's parents, so that this boy knew a great deal about their lives, knowledge he was now using to make this preposterous claim. Parker's story, supported by the supposed Matthew, by Captain Marlow, and the captured pirate Bassett, had convinced the planter, but he had visited the gaol and Matt was brought to a room for the interview. He was shocked to find Parker and Captain Marlow with his uncle, and he cried to the handsome, richly clad planter, 'Sir, why are these two here? Do you not know they are the scoundrels who are responsible for my misfortunes and who have tricked you?'

Colonel Tuke frowned, seeing a boy about his nephew's age, but a pitiful sight. Matt had suffered physically in the week he had been in the gaol, losing weight and with little opportunity to keep himself clean. He wore breeches and a shirt, both torn and dirty, and his hair had grown long and now hung in uncombed disorder. He knew now that his enemies were determined to get rid of him for ever, and that they had convinced the gaolers and officials that he was an impostor, a trickster . . . or insane. There was desperation in his eyes when he gazed at his uncle.

'It would seem one of these gentlemen has been your victim, rather than your persecutor,' the planter answered sternly. 'And the other is here to say who you are, so that you will not persist in this foolish story.'

'Aye, I can say who the rogue is, Colonel Tuke,' Parker agreed smoothly. 'I recognize him only too well. 'Tis the wretch your nephew saved at Taunton and whom I brought to Captain Marlow at Matthew's request.'

'An' I foolishly engaged,' Captain Marlow added, sounding disgusted with his own simplicity.

'That is a foul lie,' Matt retorted angrily. 'You tricked me by claiming to be Captain Howell of the *Speedwell* and I was spirited aboard the *Avon Pride*.'

Captain Marlow shook his head, watching the boy with grudging admiration.

'The swab should ha' been a play actor, Colonel,' he said. 'I've not seen better in Bristol's theatre. 'Tis as well I made for Virginia when I was taken off that island.'

'When I saved your life,' Matt flung at him contemptuously. 'You would have been thrown overboard if I had not pleaded for you.'

Captain Marlow chuckled.

'I'm beholden to ye then, lad,' he mocked, 'but it will not save yer neck. It was you passed files to the other rogues and helped them take my ship.'

'This serves no purpose' Colonel Tuke interrupted. He looked at Matt sternly. 'Why do you persist in this story, boy?' he demanded. 'It will not help you and might even anger the court against you when you come for trial. Master Parker, my agent here, has told me where you got information on my family, by questioning my two nephews. . . .'

'Ah!' Matt exclaimed. 'Where is this second nephew, sir? If he who calls himself Matt Tuke is here, where then is Peter Burdell?'

The planter looked surprised, then annoyed.

'You know well enough where he is, you wicked boy,' he retorted. 'You saw him leave with the captain of a ship bound for the East Indies, a friend of Captain Marlow who was in a tavern in Bristol.' He saw Matt was about to speak and he held a hand up. 'Do not lie any more, boy,' he commanded. 'My sister has had word from her son, Peter, after he joined this ship. He was offended because I did not invite him to Virginia with his cousin, and said he would prefer to seek his own fortune.'

Matt listened with horror, staring at Parker.

'Ye missed nothing in your plotting, you wretch,' he cried angrily.

The boy swung towards his uncle. 'My Aunt Janet will quickly settle this matter, sir,' he cried, 'if you will write to her and ask her to describe me and Peter.'

'My sister is in no condition to be troubled with your trickery,' Colonel Tuke answered. 'She has been gravely ill this past two months and I'd not cause her needless anxiety.' He paused, to take a sheet of paper from his coat pocket and hold it towards the boy. 'Did you write this, boy?'

Matt recognized the paper.

'I did, sir,' he said; ' 'tis a letter I was permitted to write to you several days ago, pleading that you come here.'

'A privilege that was urged upon your gaolers,' the planter said, 'to prove the falseness of your story. I have fifty letters from my nephew, written from England, and that scrawl is not his handwriting. I have seen his handwriting since he came here and it is the same as in the letters he wrote from England.'

'But Peter wrote all my letters,' the boy cried, a wail of

despair in his voice as he realized the trick that was being played by Parker and his cousin. 'I am a poor hand with a pen, sir, as ye see in that letter, and I had Peter write for me.' He saw the disbelief in the man's eyes and held his hands out pleadingly. 'I beg you, sir—believe me. This is the truth and these men are lying.'

'There's cunning for ye, Colonel,' Captain Marlow exclaimed admiringly. 'Had the answer quick as you like.'

'Better for himself had he applied his wits to more honest purpose,' the planter answered coldly. 'And now, I've had enough of this. I find it distasteful.' He frowned on the boy. 'I advise you to stop this stupid impersonation,' he warned. 'You have made my nephew ill with your foolishness, for he had liked you for the short time he knew you. Your ingratitude has saddened him and you show poor return for his kindnesses.'

'Why did he not come here and face me?' Matt demanded. 'Bring him, sir, and ye'll see who tells the truth. He was ever a coward and would not dare lie to my face.'

'Enough, boy,' the planter commanded angrily. 'It is enough to tell your foul lies, and I'll not have such trash insult an honest boy.' He turned to the gaoler. 'Take him back to where he came from,' he ordered angrily. 'I was foolish to come here at all.'

Matt was thrust roughly from the room and back to his cell. Bridger gazed at him in surprise when he was flung through the doorway, but Jacko nodded as though he had expected Matt to return.

'They dished ye, eh, chum,' he said huskily. 'I guessed they had. Marlow and Parker have a tight story, and wi' that traitor Bassett to back them up ye'd want more proof than yer word.' He looked at the other boy shrewdly. 'What happened, chum? Did yer uncle listen?'

Matt described what had occurred, his voice despairing. Bridger cursed indignantly at every sentence the boy spoke, but Jacko listened as though admiring the skill of Parker's trickery.

'They had ye there, chum,' he whispered, when Matt told of

the letters and handwriting. ' 'Twas that likely gave Parker the idea to start wi'. He's a cunning fox, and would see how the trick could be worked.' He looked at Matt expectantly. 'Did ye not ask for yer cousin to face ye, mate?'

'He is ill,' Matt answered, 'from knowing of my treachery.'

'By Parker's orders,' Jacko retorted. 'To keep him out of yer way, chum. But he must appear in the court when we are tried, and ye'll have him then, chum. He's a cowardly rat and will betray himself.'

But Peter did not appear at Matt's trial and the boy's claim to be the nephew of Colonel Tuke was dismissed contemptuously. When Bassett gave evidence he was asked if he knew Matt's name and he glanced at the boy furtively, then nodded.

'I heard him called Gubbins, yer honour,' he said quickly, 'an' he was Captain Marlow's cabin-boy. 'Twas him passed the files to Bridger when we was on deck one day.' Bassett paused, to lick his lips. 'They had known each other somewhere,' he added. 'Least, that is what Bridger said.'

'Ye foul and stinking rat,' the sailor roared from the dock. He jerked forward and gasped as a guard drove the butt of a pike into his back, but he could not be silenced when Parker was called to describe how he had gone to New Providence and pretended to be an agent for dishonest merchants. Bridger showed his stained teeth in a ferocious leer, watching the witness balefully.

'Mate,' the sailor called out softly when Parker had given his evidence, 'ye tricked me proper, but ye signed yer death warrant in the doin' o't. There's a thousand bold sea rovers 'll be watching for ye, who'll think it an honour to slit yer lying throat. Ye've helped to hang a lad ye swindled out of his inheritance, but ye sailed into dangerous waters when ye set yerself against the brethren of the sea. . . . If it's any comfort to young Matt Tuke, ye'll never live to share in his uncle's wealth.'

The last words were smothered in commands from the judge to silence the prisoner, and when Bridger stopped and laughed towards the Attorney-General the official glowered on him.

'I have to warn you that if you threaten a witness again,' the judge warned, 'I'll end this case and sentence you on what's been heard.'

Bridger laughed again.

'Go to it, mate,' he mocked. 'Ye've already decided we're to die. I care little for myself, for that's how a gentleman of fortune should go. . . . But let the lads go. Had it not been for that black-hearted rogue, Parker, and the fat swab of a shipmaster, who owes his life to one of the same lads, they'd not be here.'

He was silenced by painful blows at his kidneys and he fell across the front of his dock, his face twisted with pain. He straightened, gasping, and Jacko whispered hoarsely:

'Ye do no service, mate, to me or Matt. They mean to have us hung, and if we are saved it will be from our own cunning. Let them get on with it.'

So Matt heard himself sentenced to be hanged for piracy and tried to hold himself proudly as he was hustled from the dock to where an open cart waited to carry the prisoners back to the public gaol. People watched them pass, children running after the cart and screaming at them, and Sam Bridger shouted greetings to every pretty young woman.

'Show the swabs how a gentleman of fortune takes what comes,' he urged the two boys. 'Wi' an oath or a laugh, but never a whine.'

Matt could not hope to imitate the sailor's reckless defiance, and sat in the cart with head bowed, praying for courage. Jacko sat against him, watching Bridger with sardonic amusement, winking to the screaming children, while all the time his keen brain was working, seeking a loophole in this predicament.

'Mate,' he whispered to the other boy, 'cheer up. You ain't dead yet.'

'What hope have we, Jacko?' Matt asked. 'You will wish now that I had never rescued you at Taunton.'

'Mate,' Jacko whispered earnestly, 'I wouldn't have missed

what we've done, not for the chance to lift the Queen's crown. And the sport ain't finished yet.'

But Jacko's defiant courage seemed to desert him the next day, when their death warrant was read to the three condemned prisoners and they learned that they were to die in ten days' time. The warrant had been signed by Governor Spotswood and brought to the gaol by the Provost Marshal, magnificently uniformed and awe-inspiring. He was accompanied by lesser officials, soldiers, and a minister, and the three prisoners were arraigned in their cell before him. Bridger listened to the long legal phrases with a cheerful grin and Matt tried to hold himself erect and not to show the weakness he felt in his limbs. He dared not look at his companions, only at the Provost Marshal, and he did not realize anything was wrong with Jacko until he saw the black-gowned minister step forward with his arms out as though to catch something. Then Jacko moaned and fell forward, flat on his face on the stone floor of the cell, only to rear up again in a convulsive movement where his small body arched, then jerked in a horrible stiffening of the thin limbs. The boy rolled on the floor, his legs kicking, his arms twisting together unnaturally while he uttered shrill cries, his mouth gaping and his eyes seeming to bulge from their sockets. The minister was on his knees, trying to grasp the slight form, and Sam Bridger flung an oath at the still-reading Provost Marshal, then stooped to gather the boy in his arms. It was like holding an armful of fighting animals, Jacko's small fists beating at the sailor, his legs kicking.

'Easy, sprat,' Bridger gasped as he was kicked in the stomach. 'What they done, younker—scared ye?'

'Have someone bring a surgeon,' the minister cried anxiously. 'The boy has had a fit.'

'Fetch water,' Bridger shouted angrily. 'Ye've got to shock him back to his senses. . . . Get a bucket and toss it over him.'

'Oh, Sam,' Matt cried. 'You can't do that to him.'

'It's all that will stop these fits,' Bridger answered, trying to imprison Jacko's arms. 'Damme, he's strong as an ox when he gets them!'

A soldier ran into the cell, carrying a bucket and Bridger shouted for him to let it fly.

'Never mind me,' he roared. 'I been wet before.'

The water struck the struggling, screaming boy and he gave one last horrible cry and went limp, hanging across Bridger's arm as though his bones had melted. The sailor carried him to the pile of straw that was their bed, then swung on the officials.

'Now finish yer rigmarole,' he snarled, 'and get out of here. Ye can hang us as high as ye like, but we need not listen to yer bilge.'

'I have finished,' the Provost Marshall answered with as much dignity as he could summon. 'What ails this lad?'

Bridger sneered.

'Are ye blind?' he demanded. 'He's had a fit. . . . Gets them when he's scared bad. He had thought to have grown out of the affliction, but what ye've done to him here has brought them back.'

'I'll have a surgeon attend on him,' the officer said stiffly, and Bridger snorted.

'He'll be cured when ye hang him,' he said harshly. 'There's no surgeon can help him. . . . Only a dousing to shock him out o' it.'

The sailor looked down at the wet floor, shrugging his wide shoulders.

'Have one of yer lobsters fetch cloths, so we can dry our cell, f he gets more of them attacks I hopes ye'll stop it somewhere else. This place will be damp enough to give us the ague and it'll be dead pirates ye hang.'

The Provost Marshal turned away to stride from the cell, his retinue following. The minister, a young, pale-faced and earnest-looking man, turned to look at Jacko where he lay huddled and breathing thickly on the straw.

'I had meant to pray with you,' he said. 'But I will return tomorrow.'

'You do that, mate,' the sailor answered, 'and if ye can bring a plug of chewing stuff to an unfortunate sailorman ye can pray as long as ye like.'

The minister shook his head at such flippancy, then left the cell, the gaoler slamming the door shut and turning the key. Sam Bridger chuckled.

'Nicely done, sprat,' he whispered. 'But better lay where ye are for a bit. They might send a surgeon to ye.'

Matt gasped, staring at Jacko.

'He was shamming, Sam!' he exclaimed, and Bridger winked.

'Not so loud, mate,' he warned. 'Ye could spoil the neatest trick I've seen in years.' He chuckled again. 'Ye needn't ha' kicked my stomach in, sprat,' he added, 'and I was scared ye'd poke an eye out wi' them dirty paws.'

'But how will this help us?' Matt demanded, bewildered by what he had learned. 'Or will they not execute Jacko if he has fits?'

Jacko was sitting up, dark eyes gleaming with mischief. He looked immensely pleased with himself.

'Chum,' he whispered, 'ye don't get the trick. Ye heard Sam say I had to be doused when I had them fits . . . and not in the cell. We wants to see what's outside and then work out a scheme. Two or three of them attacks and I'll have this place measured like it was Cheapside. I'll find a hole where we can crawl through somewhere.'

Jacko shammed another fit while the minister was with them the next day. Again, the small figure flung itself on the cell floor, to jerk and twist into fearsome contortions, while the boy's mouth gaped and his eyes bulged in horrible grimaces that Matt could hardly believe were feigned. The minister broke off his long prayer to call for the gaoler and Sam roared for him to be carried out of the cell and doused. It took two men to hold the boy. He seemed to have the strength of a dozen men, and he scratched and kicked as he was carried through the gaol, prisoners in other cells, some of them the survivors of the *Avon Pride*'s crew who had also been sentenced to death, roaring and stamping their feet in a turmoil of noise.

'Mate,' Sam Bridger told the thoroughly unnerved preacher, 'ye scared him again. All that talk about paying for yer sins an' where he'll go if he don't repent. You want to steer easy on that tack, mate.'

'But it is my duty to prepare you for death,' the minister cried, 'to have you resign yourselves to your punishment.'

'We knows that, mate,' Bridger agreed. 'Only not every day. If you was to come, say, every second day? Ye could load aboard a full cargo o' salvation by the time we gets topped.'

Jacko was brought back to the cell, carried by a goaler and laid on the straw, where he lay looking already dead. The goaler looked down with pity in his eyes.

'Took a couple of buckets that time,' he said with rough sympathy. 'I better fetch ye some old duds to put him into.'

When he had brought a bundle of soiled and worn clothes, and was gone again, Jacko sat up. He looked a pathetic morsel, his hair like seaweed and his face seeming smaller than ever. His dark eyes gleamed with annoyance.

'This ain't going to be easy, mate,' he announced. 'There's two turnkeys inside, and one in the yard standing by a gate there, and the wall's a full ten feet high wi' nowhere to climb.'

'Did ye find where the cell keys are hung?' Bridger asked. 'If ye act bad enough next time, they'll maybe not lock the cell when they carries you out, and we can nip out and get the keys, open up the other cells and have all hands rush the turnkeys.'

'They hang them from their belts,' Jacko said disgustedly. 'An' so yer scheme ain't no good, mate. I got to have another fit and, look around some more.' The small face set stubbornly. 'I ain't never been beat yet and I ain't letting myself be now.'

But even Jacko lost his confident scorn for the goal and the gaolers as the days passed and he could discover no way to freedom. He went into his pretended fits five times in the next eight days, and returned from each attempt drenched and sulky, furious that he could find no way to get beyond the small courtyard where the guards flung water over him. His attack and their treatment had become an entertainment for the other prisoners, and an amusement for the turnkeys.

'We're going to miss yer, lad,' one of them told the glowering boy when he brought the prisoners their daily meal. 'Ain't had sport like this since I took on being a turnkey.'

Jacko spat his reply, the man grinning at the flood of oaths coming from the boy's lips.

'Reg'ler out-an'-outer,' the gaoler admired. 'I hates to think you ain't going to be with us long.'

That he was being considered an amusement infuriated the boy and he scowled and cursed when the man had gone, swearing that he would find a way out of this gaol somehow. His companions let him exhaust his spleen, both of them now convinced that they would stay where they were until they were taken out to be hanged. Their resignation infuriated Jacko, who saw it as a loss of faith in his skill. But on the day before their execution Jacko returned from another dousing with water angrily admitting defeat.

'There ain't but one way out of this hole,' he spat, 'an' that's when they takes us. It's tighter than Newgate and ye'd need wings to get away.'

Matt watched the boy sadly. He had been excited by Jacko's first attempts to find a means of escape, but as the days passed and Jacko became more and more angry and disappointed, Matt had resigned himself to his fate. He would die in this country, a shameful death as a criminal. There were nights when the boy lay shivering with fear, but during the days he hid his fears. Bridger's rough humour and jokes about their end helped to harden the boy's acceptance, and when Jacko returned to the cell on that last day Matt felt more sorry for him in his shame in being defeated than for himself.

'You have tried, Jacko', he said gratefully, 'and that you have failed is no disgrace.'

The other boy turned on him, snarling in his fury.

'A pox on ye, Matt Tuke,' he retorted. ' 'Tis no disgrace to such fools as you, but for me 'tis. That numskulls like them hulks o' turnkeys have bested me shames me afore every rogue who learns how I finished.'

Sam Bridger chuckled.

' 'Tis like a general losing a battle, mate,' he told Matt with mock solemnity, 'or Henry Morgan getting chased by a Spaniard. There's pride in what ye do, whether ye're lifting a purse or taking a prize—or even preaching a sermon like the parson what comes to see us. Jacko ain't never been bested afore and he takes it ill.'

Jacko scowled at the man.

'Ye're wrong, Sam Bridger,' he spat out. 'If it was only myself I could be out of here tonight'.

The boy stopped, his face suddenly flushed and his eyes evasive. Then he uttered an oath of disgust.

'Leave it be, mates,' he said throatily. 'I didn't mean that. Ye're right. They've beat me.'

'You are fibbing, Jacko,' Matt cried. 'You have found a way to get out. You must take it.'

'Forget it, chum,' the other boy retorted angrily, looking down to avoid Matt's eyes.

Sam Bridger was watching the boy shrewdly, admiring him.

'Ye're a true shipmate, sprat,' he said softly. 'But we ain't having it. If ye've found a way to get out of this gaol, ye'll take it. Me and Matt ain't going to let ye hang when ye could be saved.'

'I would hate that, Jacko,' Matt exclaimed. ' 'Tis bad enough that we die as we will, but it would be torture to know you also die when you could be free.'

'Spill it, younker,' Bridger demanded. 'Maybe we can help ye.'

Jacko looked up, his small face white and his eyes pleading.

'Mates,' he said pathetically, 'there ain't no way we can all get out. I thought till my mind's sore, but them cursed turnkeys is like hawks and don't make any mistakes. They been warned we ain't easy to hold, that rogue Parker even telling them I'm flamming wi' my fits.'

'Ye're dodging, mate,' Bridger chided. 'How ye going to get away? I'll haunt ye from the gallows if ye don't take yer chance.'

Jacko was looking at Matt, his eyes betraying his affection and fears.

'I wish I could get ye out, chum,' he said thickly. He paused, then shrugged his thin shoulders. 'I ain't even sure I could get away,' he said despondently, 'only there's a chance. If I was to throw a fit at night-time, when it's dark.'

'How, Jacko?' Matt asked eagerly.

'I seen how I could get the key off the turnkey's belt,' the other boy replied. 'Him that is at the yard door. If I throws myself at him when I'm flamming, then knocks over the lantern they has. They ain't never in a hurry to douse me now, getting sport out of watching me flinging myself about on the ground. If I was quick, I could get the door open maybe.'

Bridger uttered a low whistle, then shook his head.

'Ye'd have to be quick, younker,' he said, then saw the indignant expression in Jacko's face and laughed. 'Ye don't have to spit at me, lad,' he protested. 'An' maybe ye can do what ye say. 'Tis worth the trying and if ye've no better means.'

'There ain't no other way,' Jacko answered, but he was more like his old cocksure self. 'I could get that key and the swab'd never know it was gone,' he boasted, 'and if there was a yelling and banging inside the cells to upset the turnkeys, I'd have the door open and be gone.'

'Then you must try,' Matt cried. 'I'd die happier if I knew you were free, Jacko.'

'Ye might find some way of helping us, mate,' Bridger urged. 'Maybe ye could have another go at Matt's uncle. Get hold of that cousin o' his and threaten to cut his throat if he don't own up to the truth.'

Matt exclaimed excitedly, and Jacko's eyes gleamed with delight.

'Mate, ye've struck it,' he swore. 'He's a cowardly rat and I'll make him confess.'

The two boys gazed at each other eagerly, fondly, and Matt went and put his arms round the smaller boy.

'Oh, if you could, Jacko!' he cried. 'Then we could tell my uncle that Sam should be pardoned for helping us to escape from Captain Marlow.'

'Younker,' Sam Bridger interrupted, 'ain't there nothing Jacko could tell yer uncle to prove ye was his nephew? Something nobody'd know except Matt Tuke.' The man's eyes went over the boy desperately. 'Didn't ye have something? A ring maybe, or something hung round yer neck.'

Matt shook his head, smiling now. He looked down at the stained and torn breeches he had on, the soiled shirt.

'Everything I possessed was in my baggage, Sam,' he answered. 'I had a book in my riding-coat and some trifles that would prove nothing. These have all gone long ago.'

'Ye're wrong, chum,' Jacko whispered. 'I've got something that was yours.'

The boy was feeling inside the top of his breeches and the others watched him, Matt puzzled by what Jacko could mean. Then he cried out, his eyes wide and delighted as Jacko held out a small grimy hand where something lay, gleaming dully.

'Aunt Janet's medallion!' the boy cried excitedly. 'Jacko. . . . Where did you find it?'

The small face blushed for the first time since Matt had known the boy, and the dark eyes looked away guiltily.

'Ye wasn't my chum then, mate,' the throaty voice pleaded. 'I picked yer pocket when we was riding out of Taunton.' He held the silver medallion towards Matt. 'Here, mate,' he whispered, 'I allus meant ye to have it back.'

Matt held the medallion, gazing at it tenderly, remembering how and when he had recieved it.

'My aunt gave it to me when I was leaving home,' he said softly. 'It's St. Anthony . . . who always finds anything you lose.' He smiled, touching the medallion with his finger-tips. 'It had been my uncle's,' he went on. 'Aunt Janet told me to show it to him when I arrived in Virginia.'

Then a roar shattered the boy's mood of tender memories, filling the cell with jubilant sound, and Sam Bridger was racing to the thick oaken door, his fists thundering. He turned and grinned at the boys delightedly.

'Ye've got it, mate,' he shouted. 'Ye've got proof of who ye are. Yer uncle has to believe ye now.'

The small iron grille high in the door lifted and an angry face appeared.

'What's the noise for?' the gaoler demanded. 'D'ye want me to have ye chained for yer last day? I will, if ye don't lie quiet.'

'Mate,' Sam Bridger shouted into the grille, 'fetch Colonel Tuke. Tell him the lad's got proof to show now.'

The gaoler's head jerked back as Bridger's voice blasted at him, then he scowled indignantly.

'Can't ye ever learn,' he demanded furiously, 'that ye try the same trick again? I been warned ye would and ye can save yer breath. . . . Ye'll have little of it this time tomorrow.'

'Ye numskull!' Bridger roared. 'Didn't ye hear? The lad's got proof of who he is. Fetch Colonel Tuke afore I reaches out and chokes yer.'

He pushed his fingers between the bars of the grille and the gaoler struck at them with the cudgel he carried.

'Ye're mad,' he shouted, 'and if ye think I'm sending for anybody ye're the biggest fool ever. Colonel Tuke's at his plantation, twenty miles to the westward of this place. If ye want him, then ye'll fetch him yerself. Ye'll not make me as big a fool as ye are.'

The man's face disappeared, the iron cover slamming down over the grille, and Bridger was left standing, oaths pouring from him thickly.

'Lay off it, mate!' Jacko growled from behind the man. 'They

ain't going to send for nobody . . . 'cept the blacksmith to slap
irons on us. Ye heard what the swab said! Fetch him yerself . . .
an' that's what we'll do. I'll get away from this hole tonight if I
have to crawl under that door. Gimme that thing, chum. Yer
uncle'll have it by midnight.'

GOOD-BYE TO JACKO

Jacko was over-optimistic. It was far into the next morning before Colonel Tuke was awakened by a throaty voice telling him to shake the sleep out of his eyes and to come alive.

'There's yer own sword at yer ribs,' the strange voice warned. 'So sit up steady and listen.'

The planter was neither a fool nor a coward. He did as he was told, sitting up slowly, to see one of his Negro servants standing beside his bed, holding in a shaking hand a three-branched candelabrum that usually stood in the hall of the mansion. For a moment Colonel Tuke thought that his slaves had mutinied and he was to be murdered, but the servant's voice quavered another explanation.

'This young debbil, C'nol. He make me bring him to you, or he slits my froat.'

The planter turned to see who had interrupted his night, and his eyebrows lifted as he recognized the small narrow face and tangled black hair of one of the boys he had seen sentenced to death in the court-room ten days ago. Before he could speak, a thin, childlike and far from clean hand reached out and something dropped on the bed-cover between his legs.

'Mate,' the boy whispered, 'cast yer eyes on that and say what it is.'

Colonel Tuke looked down and gasped.

'My St. Anthony!' he exclaimed.

He lifted the silver medallion, turning it in his palm, then his eyes returned to the boy's face.

'Where has this come from?' he demanded. 'I have not seen it for fifteen years.'

'That's right, mate,' Jacko agreed. 'Ye gave it to yer sister when ye left England and she gave it to yer nephew, Matt Tuke.' Jacko's lips sneered. 'Not the Jack-a-dandy you calls Matt Tuke, but the right one. My chum, who's to be hung today.'

Colonel Tuke saw the candlelight flicker and he turned to the frightened Negro impatiently.

'Put that down, you half-wit,' he barked, 'and leave us.'

'He stays where he is,' Jacko ordered, 'unless ye want this blade through yer belly. I ain't having no one rouse this place and warn that scruff ye calls yer nephew that he's had his run.'

'Then sit down,' the planter told the Negro, 'before you collapse.' He turned to Jacko. 'Now, boy,' he demanded, 'how did this come into your possession? Was it stolen from my nephew?'

'Stubborn as a mule, ain't yer!' Jacko retorted. 'Did that flammer tell ye yer sister gave it to him and it was stolen from him? Ye can't lay it on me, for I never saw yer sister, and if what ye've been told is right, neither has my chum. How'd he know whose it was?'

'You mean the boy Gubbins?' Colonel Tuke asked. 'I have been troubled about that lad. I do not believe he is my nephew, but I hate to think of a boy of his age being hanged.'

'Ye might have spared a thought for me,' Jacko answered. 'I ain't much older than Matt. . . . Least I don't think so.' He watched the planter sardonically. 'Ye need a lot of convincing, mate,' he went on, 'so, ye'll get out of that bed and go and ask that rat if he lost anything on the road to Bristol. Ye don't have to tell him what it could be.'

Colonel Tuke was frowning, His nephew had never mentioned the medallion and yet, if his story were true, it could only have come into the hands of this young thief after being stolen from Matthew by the other boy. The planter felt the sword-point pressing harder against his side through the bedclothes.

'Mate,' Jacko whispered, 'there's a lad due to be swung aloft in a few hours' time. We've a ride of twenty miles to do and there ain't time to call in yer lawyers. I planned to be here hours ago, but I had to find a horse and someone to tell me how to get here . . . and it was a difficult place to find in this uncivilized country and in the dark.'

'You were in the public gaol!' Colonel Tuke exclaimed. 'I had forgotten this. How did you get permission to come here?'

Jacko grinned.

'I didn't have permission, Colonel,' he answered. 'I broke out at ten o'clock last night. Then I had to dodge round the town, looking for a horse. I got one outside a tavern, but by then the place was foul wi' redcoats and I wasted a lot of time dodging them. . . . But this ain't getting us to Williamsburg, mate. Ye can have the yarn another time.'

The planter was impressed if not admiring.

'At least you are a loyal friend to the lad,' he said, 'and I'll talk to my nephew and prove you are also the victim of a plausible young rascal.' He was getting out of the bed and now he looked at Jacko curiously. 'Why are you so sure this boy is my nephew?'

He gestured to the Negro to rise and the servant rose and held a dressing-gown for his master.

'Because he was Matt Tuke when he picked me out of trouble,' Jacko told him. 'It was me that was being whipped out of Taunton and Matt swung me aboard his horse an' got me clear. This scrag who's using his name was calling himself Peter Burdell then, and that treacherous dog Parker was calling them wi' their right names. It ain't me that's being gulled, mate.'

'This we will soon discover,' the planter said determinedly. He gestured to the Negro to pick up the candelabrum, but Jacko stopped him with a movement of the rapier.

'Ye'll carry that yerself, mate,' he said. 'We'll lock this nigger in yer room, so's he don't make a fuss. If he does, I'll come back and spike him.'

Colonel Tuke lifted the candelabrum.

'You need have no fears, boy,' he said. 'It would seem you have come here to help someone you believe, rightly or not, has been wronged. I'll make no attempt to hold you when this business is over.'

Jacko laughed, then followed the planter out of the room. They walked along a wide passage, to stop at a door.

'I'll wait here, mate,' Jacko whispered. 'You jest leave the door open, so's I hear what is said.'

Colonel Tuke opened the door and entered his nephew's room, placing the candelabrum on a table beside the bed and touching the boy's shoulder.

'Matthew,' he said, 'wake up. It is me . . . Uncle Franklyn.'

The boy awoke at once, sitting up with a startled cry that betrayed a state of nervousness. He gazed at his uncle.

'What has happened, Uncle Franklyn?' he asked dazedly. 'It is still night.'

'Aye, still night,' the man answered gravely. 'But there is something I must know, boy.'

Peter's eyes glanced towards the open door and the dark corridor, then he looked at the planter apprehensively.

'What do you mean, Uncle Franklyn?' he asked.

'There is no need to be afraid,' the man answered. 'I only wish to know if anything was stolen from you when you were travelling to Exeter, while that boy Gubbins was with you!'

Colonel Tuke could see the apprehension and evasion in the boy's eyes and he frowned.

'Come, Matthew,' he commanded, 'surely this is a simple question to answer. Was something your aunt gave you stolen from you by that young thief?'

Peter was trembling now, his eyes desperate and pleading.

'I do not understand,' he whispered. 'I cannot remember, Uncle Franklyn. Have you had a letter from my . . . my aunt?'

He crouched back as he saw the expression in his uncle's face. Colonel Tuke looked down coldly, then turned.

'Come in here, boy,' he ordered.

Jacko appeared, and Peter uttered a cry of despair, his eyes staring wildly.

Jacko was leering at the frightened boy, pointing the rapier at him.

'Well, ye dog,' he spat. 'D'ye tell the truth or do I drive this into yer lying throat?'

'He has told the truth,' Colonel Tuke said coldly. 'His guilt is in his face. I have been a fool, boy.'

'It was Parker,' Peter cried despairingly. 'It was he who made the plot.'

'And you agreed to play your part,' the planter answered sternly, 'and now ye'd have let your own cousin die so that you would gain my fortune.'

'I wanted to confess when I learned Matt was in Williamsburg,' the boy sobbed, 'but Parker said I would be hanged if I did.'

'As ye deserve, ye rat,' Jacko snarled.

'This serves no good purpose,' Colonel Tuke interrupted. 'We only torture the wretch and we must get to Williamsburg.' He looked at Jacko anxiously. 'What time is the execution to be?'

'The parson told us we leave the gaol at ten o'clock,' Jacko answered. 'They parade their victims through the town and make a ceremony of their hanging. I'm told noon is the time for topping poor devils.'

'My clock said four-thirty when we left my room,' the planter said. 'We will be in time.'

He walked to the door, ignoring the boy who now lay on his face on the bed, sobs racking him. Jacko grinned down, then smacked the rapier blade where he guessed it would be felt most. He followed the planter, who was now shouting for servants to come, and soon lights appeared, Negros carrying candles. Colonel Tuke stopped outside his bedroom, and gave orders briskly. His three fastest horses were to be saddled and brought to the door, a groom to ride with him.

'Ye'll be hungry, boy,' he told Jacko. 'Follow that servant and he will provide something. I have to write a letter to Governor Spotswood, for we cannot use time to go to him. I'll be ready to leave in ten minutes from now.'

Jacko followed the servant, to be taken to the ground floor and into a small, richly furnished room and left there. The boy's eyes searched round the furniture, gleaming with pleasure when he saw a desk. He went to it, turning down the lid and uttering a cry of satisfaction when he saw a pistol on the writing-pad. It was loaded and primed, kept there in case of robbery, and Jacko grinned as he thrust the weapon inside his breeches. He searched through several small drawers, chuckling delightedly when he found one drawer half-filled with gold coins. He scooped out the money and poured it into a pocket, thinking how horrified Matt would be if he could see. The Negro returned, carrying a tray loaded with dishes and a bottle.

When Colonel Tuke arrived the boy was smacking his lips appreciatively.

'Ye've had enough?' the planter asked. and Jacko grinned.

'I've fared worse, mate,' the boy answered.

B.J.–M

The planter did not appear to notice his pistol at the boy's waist, nor that Jacko picked up the rapier from where he had laid it on the table. They hurried to the front door, Colonel Tuke pausing there to speak to an elderly Negro.

'Joseph,' he said, 'go to my nephew's room and stay with him until my return. You'll see to it he does not leave there, nor do himself any harm.'

'Ye'll hand him over to that same fish-eyed swab who sentenced Matt,' Jacko growled.

'That I cannot do, for my sister's sake,' the man answered. 'I'll pack him home to England.'

'Then ye'll let Parker escape also,' the boy protested, but Colonel Tuke did not reply.

The horses were waiting, held by a groom. When the planter and Jacko were mounted, the groom took the third horse, Colonel Tuke handing him a letter.

'When we reach the Governor's palace you will leave us and deliver this,' he said. 'You'll see to it that he has it at once.'

Then they were off, the horses kicked into a fast pace, Jacko clinging like a limpet to his mount and using the rapier as a whip. The boy chuckled as he rode, thinking of Matt and how the boy would look when he saw his uncle. And Sam Bridger! He should have made Colonel Tuke promise to have the scar-faced sailor pardoned. Matt would plead for him. They should be in Williamsburg and at the gaol before the pirates were taken out for parading to the gallows.

Again Jacko was too optimistic. The three horsemen were still ten miles from Williamsburg when the narrow road was blocked by a squad of red-coated soldiers under the command of a sergeant. As the horses came near them a solider called out excitedly, 'That's him, sergeant . . . the rogue we are to look for. I was guard at his trial.'

The sergeant barked an order and muskets pointed at the horsemen. Colonel Tuke drew his horse up, roaring an oath.

'Out of our way, you fools,' he commanded. 'We must get to Williamsburg quickly.'

In his impatience the planter urged his horse forward, meaning to push between the ranked men, and his reins were grasped. He swore and slashed down with his riding-crop, bringing a howl of rage from the sergeant.

'Drag them off their horses,' the man shouted. 'We'll have this popinjay show respect for the Queen's uniform.'

Colonel Tuke swore as he was pulled from the saddle and Jacko drove his horse at the soldiers, screaming his fury. He struck out with the rapier, only to be grasped and flung down.

'You numskulls!' the planter roared, lashing at his captors with his riding-crop. 'I am Colonel Tuke. I'll have every man of ye whipped raw for this insult.'

' 'Tis you who'll have the whipping, fellow,' the sergeant retorted. 'Helping a pirate to escape and insulting the Queen's uniform! Ye'll walk to Williamsburg now, wi' us. We've been looking for that gaolbird.'

'I was taking him to Williamsburg,' Colonel Tuke frothed. 'We have to be there to save an innocent boy.'

'An' ye'll get there,' the sergeant told him, 'wi' us. I care little who ye are, and if that rogue cannot hang today there's more to be hanged tomorrow.' He turned to his men. 'Three of ye lead the horses,' he ordered. 'The rest of ye guard the prisoners. Drive yer butts into their ribs if they cause more trouble.'

The sergeant scowled on the irate planter, then strode away, his men poking at Colonel Tuke, Jacko, and the Negro as they followed him.

'I'll have that fool flogged until his bones show,' the planter swore as he strode beside Jacko.

'An' that won't save Matt,' the boy answered grimly. ' 'Tis now late enough and we have three hours' walking to reach the town. They'll have hanged him by then.'

But the delay was two hours. When the soldiers had marched their prisoners for six miles, an officer approached from the town, leading a squad of men. He saw Colonel Tuke and cried out in horror, and the planter poured out his wrath with oathful force. The sergeant listened, his face pale now he knew what he had done.

'You imbecile!' the officer roared at him. 'Ye'll be lucky if ye live another week. D'ye not know who you have insulted? Governor Spotswood will have ye flayed for this.'

'I've only been in the colony a fortnight,' the man cried. 'I did not know who the gentleman was, but only saw he rode with the pirate, and he was not pinioned. I thought he was being helped to escape.'

Colonel Tuke was on his horse, threatening what he would do to the unfortunate man. Jacko mounted, bringing his mount close to the planter.

'Ye waste time, mate,' he shouted impatiently. 'Time enough to punish the fool when ye've stopped the hanging. Matt will have given up hope. He'll have decided I have deserted him.'

Jacko did the other boy an injustice, for Matt was only worried for Jacko himself. If he failed to bring Colonel Tuke to the gaol, it was because he had been hurt, maybe killed, or captured. Matt's faith in the dark-haired lad was complete.

'There's still time,' he told Sam Bridger. 'If my uncle is away from the plantation, Jacko would have to find him. It may be he has had difficulty in convincing him, but I will not believe Jacko would desert me.'

'Ye have more faith in the rogue than me,' Bridger retorted. 'Yer medallion would have convinced yer uncle enough for him to have the hanging delayed.' He scowled. 'Unless that cousin of yours has thought of a plausible story.'

They were both seated on the cell floor, their legs shackled now and chained to the wall. This was punishment for their part in helping Jacko to escape, the irons secured by a gaoler who cursed and abused them as some revenge for what he had suffered from the head gaoler's tongue. Bridger had laughed as the irons were fastened to his legs, taunting the man, chuckling over what had happened.

It had been an exciting fifteen minutes, after the kicking, moaning Jacko had been carried from the cell to be doused out of his pretended fit in the gaol-yard. As soon as he was gone, Bridger had set up a roaring and urged the prisoners in other cells to kick their doors down. The building had been shaken by the noise, every prisoner shouting at the top of his voice, kicking at the cell doors until they shook on their hinges. One of the two gaolers who had carried Jacko to the yard returned to the building to threaten everyone with a flogging if they did not stop the noise, only to be spat and jeered at when he lifted a grille cover. The gaoler was still trying to quieten the prisoners when his mate ran from the yard, wanting to know if Jacko had come into the building.

'I left him, to get the bucket,' the worried gaoler exclaimed, 'and he flung himself at the turnkey in the yard, near tore him to bits wi' clawing and kicking. Then he knocked the lantern over and disappeared. He ain't in the yard.'

'And he didn't come back here,' he was told.

The prisoners who heard the conversation set up a cheer, yelling encouragement to the boy wherever he might be. Then they heard the turnkey calling for the two other guards and saying his key had been taken from his belt. Pandemonium broke out, the prisoners yelling jubilantly and mocking the gaolers. They were subdued only when soldiers arrived, threatening to fire through the grilles.

Jacko was gone and soon gaolers guarded by redcoats were in the cells, shackling the prisoners, and being taunted.

Matt and Sam Bridger had been delighted, admiring the escaped boy, and telling each other that he would reach Colonel Tuke in a few hours and Matt would be freed before daylight. But daylight came and Colonel Tuke had not arrived to save his nephew. A gaoler, still smarting under the tongue-lashing he had received for letting Jacko get away, brought them a meagre breakfast. When Bridger snarled that condemned men should have better food on their last day, he was told he should have thought of this before helping in an escape. It was partly his annoyance in not being given this last privilege that made Bridger spit out angrily against Jacko, and Matt made his defence of the other boy.

Not until the minister arrived to pray with them for the last time did Matt begin to lose his confidence and to glance at Bridger worriedly. The man winked, assuring him that they were not dead yet.

'Ye're wasting yer breath, cully,' he told the minister. 'The boy ain't to die. There's proof of who he is gone to Colonel Tuke and he'll be here soon.'

The young minister shook his head sorrowfully, chiding them gently for continuing their deception and not accepting their fate with resignation and humility. Matt knelt with the preacher, but prayed for Jacko's safety and the success of his mission. When the minister had gone, to visit four other pirates who were to be hanged with Matt and Bridger, the sailor looked at the boy unhappily.

'The chit's betrayed ye,' he said gently, 'or he's failed with yer uncle. They'd have been here by now if all was well.'

This time Matt did not reply, only gazed at the man and knew himself afraid. When horses' hoofs clapped on the road outside the gaol and they heard the rumble of wheels Bridger reached over and gripped the boy comfortingly.

'That's the cart come to carry us to the gallows, younker,' he said. 'Don't let the swabs see ye're scared.'

'But I am, Sam,' Matt cried. 'Terribly afraid.'

'Who isn't, mate?' the man answered. "We'll all be shaking in our shoes, but there's them come to watch a man cringe and ye have to try and laugh at them.' He shrugged his wide shoulders 'What's it matter anyhow, younker? Ye die sooner or later, at the end of a rope or in yer bed. . . . Ye jest try and go like a true man.'

When gaolers arrived, escorted by soldiers, Matt's face was pale, but he held himself proudly while the chain securing him to the wall was struck away and shackles were fastened to his wrists. Bridger joked with the guards, asking if a good crowd had gathered to see how bold pirates died. When they shuffled out of their cells he hailed the four other condemned men boisterously, calling back to other prisoners, who roared from their cells and wished them a good passage. Matt kept close to the man, striving for courage. They were taken from the gaol to where a high-sided, open, two-wheeled cart waited, the driver seated in front and a powerful-looking farm horse in the shafts. A procession had formed, the Provost Marshal in front, carrying the silver oar Matt had seen in the court-room. Lesser officials walked behind the magnificently attired Provost Marshal, soldiers formed up on either side of the cart and behind it, while the pale-faced young minister walked close to the prisoners, intoning prayers. The pirates grinned down from their height on the people who had come to see them, though here the crowd was small. The towns-people were gathered outside the town, nearer to the gallows and around them, making an outing of this entertainment.

Now, at a signal from the Provost Marshal, the procession started, children running outside the lines of soldiers, screaming and leaping. The pirates saluted the women they saw, joked with their audience as the cart rumbled through the wide straight streets of Williamsburg. Matt, standing against Bridger, gazed about him and over the heads of the crowd, seeking hopefully for Jacko and Colonel Tuke. But he did not now believe he was to be rescued from this shameful and terrifying death.

'Look, mate,' a pirate shouted. 'They've done us proud. We're having proper gallows and not being slung off this craft!'

He raised his shackled arms to point and they all saw the grim scene, a row of six gallows, ropes already formed into nooses dangling from them. A long wooden platform had been erected under the gallows, red-coated soldiers standing on them, and Matt shivered.

'What happens, Sam?' he asked in a low whisper. 'Do we have to jump off the platform?'

'That's it, younker,' the man answered, making his reply gruffly. 'But the parson has his say first, then we're permitted to address the crowd, and tell 'em how sorry we are we didn't live honest. Then ye jumps, mate, and if ye don't they shoves ye off!' He looked at the boy approvingly. 'Ye're holding yerself like a proper man, younker,' he praised, 'so ye'll jump and show them ye went boldly.'

Matt dared not speak again, for his throat was thick with horror and the shame of this moment. He could see people all round the cart now and in front of it, hundreds of faces and eyes staring up at him, curious and some with an awful greediness in them. A few looked sympathetically at him as they discovered his youthfulness and a woman cried encouragingly. The pirates still shouted to the now dense crowd, promising good entertainment, making their grim jokes, and people were laughing, a few slatterns throwing kisses. When Matt heard louder shouts, yells of abuse and people seeming to jostle more he thought it only an increase of excitement now the gallows was so near. He looked over the crowd, to the fields beyond, thinking that this would be his last sight of a world he had enjoyed for so few years. He suddenly remembered the fields outside Exeter and felt tears flowing, as Sam Bridger uttered a loud oath at his ear and gripped the boy fiercely.

'Younker!' the man shouted. 'Ye're safe. Yer uncle and Jacko are come.'

He spun the boy round, facing behind the cart, and Matt saw the two riders. They were only a few hundred yards away, Colonel Tuke in front, striking down at the people who did not give way. Jacko looked like a monkey on his horse, and like the planter he was striking at those who did not leap aside, slashing at backs and heads with the thin rapier blade. The thin dark face was twisted into an expression of fury, the dark eyes gleaming with excitement, and even as Matt looked round, the familiar throaty voice screamed out oaths and abuse at someone who clutched at the horse's bridle. Sam Bridger roared a greeting, laughing as he watched the boy slashing at the crowd. The other pirates were

cheering, shouting for Jacko to split their thick heads if they didn't jump. The boy heard them and looked up, grinning widely and waving the rapier.

The disturbance the riders were causing was making the crowd sway and crush away from the road, the noise spreading outward as people protested at being trampled on. The officials walking in front of the cart were turning round, the soldiers trying to restrain their curiosity and look ahead. Colonel Tuke rose in his stirrups, roaring powerfully and demanding that the Provost Marshal be told to stop.

Matt was laughing, gripping Bridger's arm and crying that they were saved and the man was laughing with him.

'Good luck to ye, younker,' he shouted, 'and ye can tell Jacko I shouldn't ha' said he'd betrayed ye.'

'You can tell him yourself, Sam,' Matt cried. 'My uncle will have you pardoned now he knows what a wretch Captain Marlow is and that it is thanks to you I escaped him.'

Bridger laughed again.

'I've little hope, younker,' he said, 'for I was the cause of men being slaughtered at that island. Governor Spotswood would need a deal of convincing afore he'll spare the likes of me.'

'Matthew! Matthew!' Colonel Tuke sang out then, and the boy turned to see his uncle riding close to the cart now, forcing past the soldiers. 'Ye're safe, child,' the planter called. 'I've learned the truth.'

Jacko was on the other side of the cart, laughing throatily, his dark eyes gleaming. Bridger shouted to him and the boy winked. His horse was forcing the soldiers out of line, the crowd pressing closer and shouting that the pirates were not to hang and had been pardoned. For the moment the procession was in disorder, the Provost Marshal trying to make himself heard as he demanded to be told who had caused this interruption. Jacko was kicking his horse ahead, and now his arm rose and came down, the rapier blade descending on the horse's hind-quarters. It reared to the pain of the blow, its driver hauling back on the reins. Sam Bridger laughed thunderously, his arms swinging and knocking the carter backward and into the cart, while Bridger grasped at the reins, yelling as the horse reared and frightened officials leapt aside from its hoofs. Jacko was screaming, thrashing at the horse, and it brought its front feet down with a clash and bolted, people screaming and scattering from its path.

The suddenness of Jacko's action brought it success. With the crowd's attention diverted from the prisoners to the handsome, commanding figure of Colonel Tuke and his demand to stop the execution, no one noticed the small boy until he had acted. When the horse reared its front feet to his painful blow, fear of being struck made people crush and back away, the soldiers being jostled with the crowd. Then the cart was jolting as the horse bolted, Jacko riding alongside and slashing at it while Bridger beat with the reins on its back. No one stood in its way and the road was clear as its hoofs thundered and it raced to escape the blows being showered on its hind-quarters by a screaming demon. The soldiers on the gallows platform could only gape as they watched the prisoners being borne past them, and only one person attempted to stop the escape. Captain Marlow, come to gloat at his enemies, flung people aside in his fury, to clear a way. He ran into the roadway, his arms waving. Bridger saw him and roared delightedly, tugging on a rein to drive the maddened horse at the shipmaster. He saw his danger and turned to run, then was flung violently to the ground as a cart shaft struck him. He screamed, then the cart tilted as the wheel went over the huge body, and Bridger was laughing.

'There's no pursuit, mate,' a pirate shouted. 'Ye've a clear road to the coast.'

Matt, clinging to the front of the cart, dazed and bewildered by what was happening, looked round. The road was empty, except where the crowd milled and shouted close to the gallows. A musket-shot sounded, but the ball came nowhere near the fleeing pirates. Jacko laughed, grinning towards Matt.

'Chum,' he screamed, 'ye get me more fun than anybody. I hates to be leaving ye.'

'We best find a way off this road,' a pirate shouted. 'There's forest ahead, mate and ye'd best turn into it. They be after us when they get their wits back.'

'I know the place,' another called. 'I was brought here as a servant. Ye can pass through that wood and there's a farm beyond where we'll find tools and get rid of them irons.'

The horse was still racing wildly, neck stretched and nostrils dilated, but its pace was slowing and Bridger was handling the reins skilfully.

'Damme, mate!' one of the pirates exclaimed 'Ye handle this craft like the skipper of a Bristol flyer.'

'I'm Somerset-born,' Bridger boasted, 'and learned to steer a horse afore I ever tucked a long splice.'

He was soothing the animal with his handling of the reins, bringing it under control, and by the time they were near the trees the hoofs were beating less wildly, though the horse strode on powerfully. Jacko had dropped behind, looking round for signs of pursuit, but the road was empty, a small hill hiding the gallows and the people there. Sam Bridger hauled on a rein, turning the horse off the road and among trees, then lay back, bringing the panting animal to a stop.

'Ye leave us here, younker,' he told Matt. 'And there's no time for long farewells.'

'But you need not run away, Sam,' the boy cried. 'My uncle will find you a pardon.'

Bridger laughed.

'I'd toss it back in Spotswood's face,' he declared. 'I've no fancy for a merchantman's ten shilling a month. . . . So, out wi' ye, lad. We'll not strain our luck wi' waiting.'

Matt gazed at the man dismally, then pushed past the other men and was lowered to the ground over the rear of the cart. Bridger made a clucking sound and the horse went ahead, the pirates calling back good-byes. Jacko still sat his horse, grinning down at Matt.

'You will come with me, Jacko?' the boy pleaded. 'I have not thanked ye properly and I will hate it if you are not with me.'

Jacko chuckled, his eyes going over the other boy humorously.

'Chum,' he said in the voice Matt Tuke would never forget, 'I'd die outa weariness in a place like that. They've got it laid out like a graveyard, all squares and flowers wi' the houses stuck like tombstones. Not a smell in the place, 'cept flowers, and what smoke they makes gets away before it can get near a throat.'

Matt opened his mouth to protest, then they both heard the beat of horses' hoofs and Jacko jerked his own horse round.

'Mate,' he whispered, 'good luck, and I'll come and visit ye one day . . . through a window.'

Then he was gone and Matt was staring helplessly at the horse's hind-quarters. The cart had already disappeared among the trees and Jacko's horse, the tiny figure crouched on its back, was already being hidden. The boy turned and hobbled awkwardly towards the road. Colonel Tuke saw him, and uttered a cry, lying back on his horse and bringing it to a sudden, sliding stop. He leapt from the saddle, to take the boy in his arms.

'I am sorry, Matthew,' Colonel Tuke said.

Matt laughed, more from excitement than merriment.

'Where is the other boy, Matthew?' Colonel Tuke asked, looking past the boy to where he saw wheel-tracks on the grass. 'I would like to do something for him.'

Matt remembered and looked alarmed.

'You can, Uncle Franklyn,' he cried. 'Carry me away from this place before others come. And let me tell them I was flung from the cart and that it continued on the road.'

The man laughed, nodding his head.

'We can do that, Matthew,' he said gently, 'but let us make this the last falsehood. I have had enough lies from others.'

He mounted, then bent down and lifted the boy in front of the saddle, to sit sideways because of his shackles. Then the planter turned the horse and rode towards Williamsburg.